PE
SECRETS AN

Bernard Mac Laverty w
ten years as a
English at Queen's   moved to Scotland and
taught for a number of years. He now writes full-time and lives
in Glasgow with his wife and four children.

Secrets and Other Stories, his first book, won a Scottish Arts
Council Book Award, as did *Lamb*, *A Time to Dance* and *Cal*.
Lamb was runner-up to the Guardian Fiction Prize, and *A Time
to Dance* won the literature prize in the *Sunday Independent*'s
Annual Arts Award. Both *Lamb* and *Cal* have been made into
successful films. He is also the author of *The Great Profundo and
Other Stories*.

Bernard Mac Laverty's work has received widespread ac-
claim. The *Spectator* said of *Cal*: 'Mr Mac Laverty describes the
sad, straitened, passionate lives of his characters with tremen-
dously moving skill'; and the *Daily Telegraph* commented of
Lamb, 'The narrative power is considerable; the compassion re-
markable.' The *New Statesman* called *A Time to Dance* 'A splen-
did collection of short stories . . . Mac Laverty is one of the best
practitioners of the genre we have.'

SECRETS

AND
OTHER STORIES

Bernard Mac Laverty

PENGUIN BOOKS

PENGUIN BOOKS

Published by the Penguin Group
Penguin Books Ltd, 27 Wrights Lane, London W8 5TZ, England
Viking Penguin, a division of Penguin Books USA Inc.
375 Hudson Street, New York, New York 10014, USA
Penguin Books Australia Ltd, Ringwood, Victoria, Australia
Penguin Books Canada Ltd, 2801 John Street, Markham, Ontario, Canada L3R 1B4
Penguin Books (NZ) Ltd, 182–190 Wairau Road, Auckland 10, New Zealand

Penguin Books Ltd, Registered Offices: Harmondsworth, Middlesex, England

First published by The Blackstaff Press 1977
with the assistance of the Arts Council of Northern Ireland
This edition first published by Allison & Busby
and by The Blackstaff Press 1984
Published in Penguin Books 1990
3 5 7 9 10 8 6 4 2

Some of these stories have been published or broadcast by
the following: *Irish Press, Honest Ulsterman, Caret,
Fortnight*, BBC Radio and TV, RTE Radio, *Winter's Tales from Ireland 2*
(Gill and Macmillan), *New Irish Writers* (Dtv Zweisprachig),
Soundings 3 (Blackstaff Press), *Scottish Short Stories 1977* (Collins).

Printed in England by Clays Ltd, St Ives plc

Contents

for Madeline

The Exercise

'We never got the chance,' his mother would say to him. 'It wouldn't have done me much good but your father could have bettered himself. He'd be teaching or something now instead of serving behind a bar. He could stand up with the best of them.'

Now that he had started grammar school Kevin's father joined him in his work, helping him when he had the time, sometimes doing the exercises out of the text books on his own before he went to bed. He worked mainly from examples in the Maths and Language books or from previously corrected work of Kevin's. Often his wife took a hand out of him, saying 'Do you think you'll pass your Christmas Tests?'

When he concentrated he sat hunched at the kitchen table, his non-writing hand shoved down the back of his trousers and his tongue stuck out.

'Put that thing back in your mouth,' Kevin's mother would say, laughing. 'You've a tongue on you like a cow.'

His father smelt strongly of tobacco for he smoked both a pipe and cigarettes. When he gave Kevin money for sweets he'd say, 'You'll get sixpence in my coat pocket on the bannisters.'

Kevin would dig into the pocket deep down almost to his elbow and pull out a handful of coins speckled with bits of yellow and black tobacco. His father also smelt of porter, not his breath, for he never drank but from his clothes and Kevin thought it mixed nicely with his grown up smell. He loved to smell his pyjama jacket and the shirts that he left off for washing.

Once in a while Kevin's father would come in at six o'clock, sit in his armchair and say, 'Slippers'.

'You're not staying in, are you?' The three boys shouted and danced around, the youngest pulling off his big boots, falling back on the floor as they came away from his feet, Kevin, the eldest, standing on the arm of the chair to get the slippers down from the cupboard.

'Some one of you get a good shovel of coal for that fire,' and they sat in the warm kitchen doing their homework, their father reading the paper or moving about doing some job that their mother had been at him to do for months. Before their bedtime he would read the younger ones a story or if there were no books in the house at the time he would choose a piece from the paper. Kevin listened with the others although he pretended to be doing something else.

But it was not one of those nights. His father stood shaving with his overcoat on, a very heavy navy overcoat, in a great hurry, his face creamed thick with white lather. Kevin knelt on the cold lino of the bathroom floor, one elbow leaning on the padded seat of the green wicker chair trying to get help with his Latin. It was one of those exercises which asked for the nominative and genitive of: an evil deed, a wise father and so on.

'What's the Latin for "evil"?'

His father towered above him trying to get at the mirror, pointing his chin upwards scraping underneath.

'Look it up at the back.'

Kevin sucked the end of his pencil and fumbled through the vocabularies. His father finished shaving, humped his back and spluttered in the basin. Kevin heard him pull the plug and the final gasp as the water escaped. He groped for the towel then genuflected beside him drying his face.

'Where is it?' He looked down still drying slower and slower, meditatively until he stopped.

'I'll tell you just this once because I'm in a hurry.'

Kevin stopped sucking the pencil and held it poised, ready and wrote the answers with great speed into his jotter as his father called them out.

'Is that them all?' his father asked, draping the towel over the side of the bath. He leaned forward to kiss Kevin but he lowered his head to look at something in the book. As he rushed down the stairs he shouted back over his shoulder.

'Don't ever ask me to do that again. You'll have to work them out for yourself.'

He was away leaving Kevin sitting at the chair. The towel edged its way slowly down the side of the bath and fell on the floor. He got up and looked in the wash-hand basin. The bottom was covered in short black hairs, shavings. He drew a white path through them with his finger. Then he turned and went down the stairs to copy the answers in ink.

Of all the teachers in the school Waldo was the one who commanded the most respect. In his presence nobody talked, with the result that he walked the corridors in a moat of silence. Boys seeing him approach would drop their voices to a whisper and only when he was out of earshot would they speak normally again. Between classes there was always five minutes uproar. The boys wrestled over desks, shouted, whistled, flung books while some tried to learn their nouns, eyes closed, feet tapping to the rhythm of declensions. Others put frantic finishing touches to last night's exercise. Some minutes before Waldo's punctual arrival, the class quietened. Three rows of boys, all by now strumming nouns, sat hunched and waiting.

Waldo's entrance was theatrical. He strode in with strides as long as his soutane would permit, his books clenched in his left hand and pressed tightly against his chest. With his right hand he swung the door behind him, closing it with a crash. His eyes raked the class. If, as occasionally happened, it did not close properly he did not turn from the class but backed slowly against the door snapping it shut with his behind. Two strides brought him to the rostrum. He cracked his books down with an explosion and made a swift palm upward gesture.

Waldo was very tall, his height being emphasised by the soutane, narrow and tight-fitting at the shoulders, sweeping down like a bell to the floor. A row of black gleaming buttons bisected him from floor to throat. When he talked his Adam's apple hit against the hard, white Roman collar and created in Kevin the same sensation as a fingernail scraping down the blackboard. His face was sallow and immobile. (There was a rumour that he had a glass eye but no-one knew which. Nobody could look at him long enough because to meet his stare was to invite a question.) He abhorred slovenliness. Once when presented with an untidy exercise book, dog-eared with a tea ring on the cover, he picked it up, the corner of one leaf between his finger and thumb, the pages splaying out like a fan, opened the window and dropped it three floors to the ground. His own neatness became exaggerated when he was at the board, writing in copperplate script just large enough for the boy in the back row to read — geometrical columns of declined nouns defined by exact, invisible margins. When he had finished he would set the chalk down and rub the used finger and thumb together with the same action he used after handling the host over the paten.

The palm upward gesture brought the class to its feet and they said the Hail Mary in Latin. While it was being said all eyes looked down because they knew if they looked up Waldo was bound to be staring at them.

'Exercises.'

When Waldo was in a hurry he corrected the exercises verbally, asking one boy for the answers and then asking all those who got it right to put up their hands. It was four for anyone who lied about his answer and now and then he would take spot checks to find out the liars.

'Hold it, hold it there,' he would say and leap from the rostrum, moving through the forest of hands and look at each boy's book, tracing out the answer with the tip of his cane. Before the end of the round and while his attention was on one book a few hands would be lowered quietly. Today he was in a hurry. The atmosphere was tense as he looked from one boy to another, deciding who would start.

'Sweeny, we'll begin with you.' Kevin rose to his feet, his finger trembling under the place in the book. He read the first answer and looked up at Waldo. He remained impassive. He would let someone while translating unseens ramble on and on with great imagination until he faltered, stopped and admitted that he didn't know. Then and only then would he be slapped.

'Two, nominative. *Sapienter Pater.*' Kevin went on haltingly through the whole ten and stopped, waiting for a comment from Waldo. It was a long time before he spoke. When he did it was with bored annoyance.

'Every last one of them is wrong.'

'But sir, Father, they couldn't be wr . . .' Kevin said it with such conviction, blurted it out so quickly that Waldo looked at him in surprise.

'Why not?'

'Because my . . .' Kevin stopped.

'Well?' Waldo's stone face resting on his knuckles. 'Because my what?'

It was too late to turn back now.

'Because my father said so,' he mumbled very low, chin on chest.

'Speak up, let us all hear you.' Some of the boys had heard and he thought they sniggered.

'Because my father said so.' This time the commotion in the class was obvious.

'And where does your father teach Latin?' There was no escape. Waldo had him. He knew now there would be an exhibition for the class. Kevin placed his weight on his arm and felt his tremble communicated to the desk.

'He doesn't, Father.'

'And what does he do?'

Kevin hesitated, stammering,

'He's a barman.'

'A barman!' Waldo mimicked and the class roared loudly.

'*Quiet.*' He wheeled on them. 'You, Sweeny. Come out here.' He reached inside the breast of his soutane and with a flourish produced a thin yellow cane, whipping it back and forth, testing it.

Kevin walked out to the front of the class, his face fiery red, the blood throbbing in his ears. He held out his hand. Waldo raised it higher, more to his liking, with the tip of the cane touching the underside of the upturned palm. He held it there for some time.

'If your brilliant father continues to do your homework for you, Sweeny, you'll end up a barman yourself.' Then he whipped the cane down expertly across the tips of his fingers and again just as the blood began to surge back into them. Each time the cane in its follow-through cracked loudly against the skirts of his soutane.

'You could have made a better job of it yourself. Other hand.' The same ritual of raising and lowering the left hand with the tip of the cane to the desired height. 'After all, I have taught you some Latin.' *Crack.* 'It would be hard to do any worse.'

Kevin went back to his place resisting a desire to hug his hands under his armpits and stumbled on a schoolbag jutting into the aisle as he pushed into his desk. Again Waldo looked round the class and said, 'Now we'll have it *right* from someone.'

The class continued and Kevin nursed his fingers, out of the fray.

As the bell rang Waldo gathered up his books and said, 'Sweeny, I want a word with you outside. Ave Maria, gratia plena . . . .' It was not until the end of the corridor that Waldo turned to face him. He looked at Kevin and maintained his silence for a moment.

'Sweeny, I must apologise to you.' Kevin bowed his head. 'I meant your father no harm — he's probably a good man, a very good man.'

'Yes, sir,' said Kevin. The pain in his fingers had gone.

'Look at me when I'm talking, please.' Kevin looked at his collar, his Adam's apple, then his face. It relaxed for a fraction and Kevin thought he was almost going to smile, but he became efficient, abrupt again.

'All right, very good, you may go back to your class.'

'Yes Father,' Kevin nodded and moved back along the empty corridor.

Some nights when he had finished his homework early he would go down to meet his father coming home from work.

12

It was dark, October, and he stood close against the high wall at the bus-stop trying to shelter from the cutting wind. His thin black blazer with the school emblem on the breast pocket and his short grey trousers, both new for starting grammar school, did little to keep him warm. He stood shivering, his hands in his trouser pockets and looked down at his knees which were blue and marbled, quivering uncontrollably. It was six o'clock when he left the house and he had been standing for fifteen minutes. Traffic began to thin out and the buses became less regular, carrying fewer and fewer passengers. There was a moment of silence when there was no traffic and he heard a piece of paper scraping along on pointed edges. He kicked it as it passed him. He thought of what had happened, of Waldo and his father. On the first day in class Waldo had picked out many boys by their names.

'Yes, I know your father well,' or 'I taught your elder brother. A fine priest he's made. Next.'

'Sweeny, Father.'

'Sweeny? Sweeny? — You're not Dr John's son, are you?'

'No Father.'

'Or anything to do with the milk people?'

'No Father.'

'Next.' He passed on without further comment.

Twenty-five past six. Another bus turned the corner and Kevin saw his father standing on the platform. He moved forward to the stop as the bus slowed down. His father jumped lightly off and saw Kevin waiting for him. He clipped him over the head with the tightly rolled newspaper he was carrying.

'How are you big lad?'

'All right,' said Kevin shivering. He humped his shoulders and set off beside his father, bumping into him uncertainly as he walked.

'How did it go today?' his father asked.

'All right.' They kept silent until they reached the corner of their own street.

'What about the Latin?'

Kevin faltered, feeling a babyish desire to cry.

'How was it?'

'OK. Fine.'

'Good. I was a bit worried about it. It was done in a bit of a rush. Son, your Da's a genius.' He smacked him with the paper again. Kevin laughed and slipped his hand into the warmth of his father's overcoat pocket, deep to the elbow.

A Rat and Some Renovations

Almost every one in Ireland must have experienced American visitors or, as we called them, 'The Yanks'. Just before we were visited for the first time, my mother decided to have the working kitchen modernised. We lived in a terrace of dilapidated Victorian houses whose front gardens measured two feet by the breadth of the house. The scullery, separated from the kitchen by a wall, was the same size as the garden, and just as arable. When we pulled out the vegetable cupboard we found three or four potatoes which had fallen down behind and taken root. Ma said, 'God, if the Yanks had seen that.'

She engaged the workmen early so the job would be finished and the newness worn off by the time the Yanks arrived. She said she wouldn't like them to think that she got it done up just for them.

The first day the workmen arrived they demolished the wall, ripped up the floor and left the cold water tap hanging four feet above a bucket. We didn't see them again for three weeks. Grandma kept trying to make excuses for them, saying that it was very strenuous work. My mother however managed to get them back and they worked for three days, erecting a sink unit and leaving a hole for the outlet pipe. It must have been through this hole that the rat got in.

The first signs were discovered by Ma in the drawer of the new unit. She called me and said, 'What's those?' I looked and saw six hard brown ovals trundling about the drawer.

'Ratshit,' I said. Ma backed disbelievingly away, her hands over her mouth, repeating, 'It's mouse, it's mouse, it must be

15

mouse.

The man from next door, a Mr Frank Twoomey, who had lived most of his life in the country, was called — he said from the size of them, it could well be a horse. At this my mother took her nightdress and toothbrush and moved in with an aunt across the street, leaving the brother and myself with the problem. Armed with a hatchet and shovel we banged and brattled the cupboards, then when we felt sure it was gone we blocked the hole with hardboard and sent word to Ma to return, that all was well.

It was after two days safety that she discovered the small brown bombs again. I met her with her nightdress under her arm, in the path. She just said, 'I found more,' and headed for her sister's.

That evening it was Grandma's suggestion that we should borrow the Grimleys' cat. The brother was sent and had to pull it from beneath the side-board because it was very shy of strangers. He carried it across the road and the rat-killer was so terrified of the traffic and Peter squeezing it that it peed all down his front. By this time Ma's curiosity had got the better of her and she ventured from her sister's to stand pale and nervous in our path. The brother set the cat down and turned to look for a cloth to wipe himself. The cat shot past him down the hall, past Ma who screamed, 'Jesus, the rat', and leapt into the hedge. The cat ran until a bus stopped it with a thud. The Grimleys haven't spoken to us since.

Ma had begun to despair. 'What age do rats live to?' she asked. 'And what'll we do if it's still here when the Yanks come?' Peter said that they loved pigs in the kitchen.

The next day we bought stuff, pungent like phosphorous and spread it on cubes of bread. The idea of this stuff was to roast the rat inside when he ate it so that he would drink himself to death.

'Just like Uncle Matt,' said Peter. He tactlessly read out the instructions to Grandma who then came out in sympathy with the rat. Ma thought it may have gone outside, so to make sure, we littered the yard with pieces of bread as well. In case it didn't work Ma decided to do a novena of masses so she got up the next morning and on the driveway to the chapel which runs along the back of our house she noticed six birds with their feet in the air, stone dead.

Later that day the rat was found in the same condition on the kitchen floor. It was quickly buried in the dust-bin using the shovel as a hearse. The next day the workmen came, finished the job, and the Yanks arrived just as the paint was drying.

They looked strangely out of place with their brown, leathery faces, rimless glasses and hat brims flamboyantly large, as we met them at the boat . . . Too summery by half, against the dripping eaves of the sheds at the dock-yard. At home by a roaring fire on a July day, after having laughed a little at the quaintness of the taxi, they exchanged greetings, talked about family likenesses, jobs, and then dried up. For the next half hour the conversation had to be manufactured, except for a comparison of education systems which was confusing and therefore lasted longer. Then everything stopped.

The brother said, 'I wouldn't call this an embarrassing silence.'

They all laughed, nervously dispelling the silence but not the embarrassment.

Ma tried to cover up. 'Would yous like another cup of cawfee?' Already she had begun to pick up the accent. They agreed and the oldish one with the blue hair followed her out to the kitchen.

'Gee, isn't this madern,' she said.

Ma, untacking her hand from the paint on the drawer, said, 'Yeah, we done it up last year.'

St Paul Could Hit the Nail
on the Head

All that afternoon Mary's world seemed to be falling apart at the seams. Each time she slipped out of the room she rolled the whites of her eyes to heaven. She kept rushing into the kitchen and talking in spikey whispers to the children, buttoning up their overcoats or giving them biscuits and drinks of water. She had managed to push the two boys, Rodney and John, out on to the street to play but the girls still hung about, afraid they would miss something. Now she came out again and stopped at the threshold. Deirdre, at two the youngest, said she was making the dinner out of cornflakes and HP sauce, sitting on her behind slopping the mess over the lip of the dish onto the floor. Mary whipped the dish from her and shook her by the shoulders, then tried to drown her screeches by shushing her.

'Patricia, take that Deirdre out of my sight, up the stairs, anywhere . . . and wash her face while you're there.'

Patricia, seven years old and the eldest, led her snivelling sister up the stairs. Mary walking down the hall saw Deirdre's white knickers, flannel grey from sitting on the floor, disappear round the stair head. She went into the front room balancing the scones on a plate.

Father Malachy, a distant cousin, who had a parish somewhere in the depths of Co Monaghan, sat firmly in the chair in the corner sipping his tea from a china cup. Due to his worsening Parkinson's Disease, it rattled every time he replaced it on the matching china saucer. He came to Belfast every year in early summer, would visit Mary for about an hour then go

18

on to stay with Jimmy Brankin for the rest of the week. He had arrived sometime just before dinner and Mary had opened the door to him, squinting against the sun.

'Ach, it's you Father Malachy, come in, come in.'

The old priest removed his hat politely as he stepped into the hallway. He had a small navy blue suitcase worn through to the brown cardboard at a point on its flank where his leg constantly rubbed against it as he walked. He set it down on the quiet carpet of the hallway and shuffled into the front room. There were clothes strewn over the floor, on the backs of chairs. A pair of trousers partially obscured the face of the morning-dead TV.

'Sit down here, Father,' said Mary, clearing a chair and throwing the things on to the floor. 'The place is in a mess. Why didn't you drop me a line to say you were coming. O God, what a mess.'

'Now, you know as well as I do there's no need to worry about that. Where do you think I was reared?'

Just then Mary noticed the pot with Deirdre's load in it and got it out of the room as fast as she could, shielding it from him with her body and saying that he must want a cup of tea after the long journey. While the kettle was coming to the boil she took off her apron, combed her hair and took time to wash her face for the first time that day. She paraded in with the tea on the tray feeling a changed woman.

'I'm sorry, Father, I never even asked you to take off your coat.'

'No, no, I'll not stay that long,' he said.

That was three hours ago. In the meantime he had refused dinner but took two bowls of soup with several potatoes 'smashed' in it. He was now in his third bout of tea drinking and had asked for another scone with raspberry jam. Mary offered him one from the plate and he ate it noisily, not bothering to close his mouth when he chewed. He had picked a spot somewhere about the level of the pelmet and stared fixedly at it most of the day. He seemed to use it as an excuse for not talking, as if it were a TV programme and he didn't like to interrupt. It meant Mary could stare at him without being offensive. He had sunk deeper into the chair, his coat ruffling up at the back. Dandruff speckled his clerical black yet he had lost little of his white hair. His hands, except for the two yellow-brown nicotine fingers, had the whiteness of someone who had been in bed sick for a long time. Dusting the scone flour from his fingers, he steadied their tremor by joining them firmly at the tips and said, 'While you were out I was noseying around. It's a nice house you've bought. This room is lovely.'

'Oh God, what a mess it was in this morning. I'm inclined to let things slide.'

'Everything you have is good,' he said, his white hands searching the texture of the leather arms of his chair.

'Good?'

'Yes,' said Father Malachy, 'Expensive . . . The contracting must be going well with Sam.'

'Oh yes. He's doing well. Demolition's the thing at the moment. They're knocking down the half of Belfast.'

'Is that right now?'

'Slum clearance.'

They lapsed into silence again.

Mary had gone down one day with the boys to see Sam and had watched the business of devastation. Bulldozers snarled in, crashing through kitchen walls, teetering staircases, leaving bedrooms exposed. They took great bites of the house then spilled the gulp into the back of a waiting lorry, the mandible unhinging at the back rather than the front. Mary felt she shouldn't look, seeing the choice of wallpapers: pink rosebuds, scorned in her own family, faded flowers, patterns modern a generation ago. She felt it was too private. She rounded up the boys, 'Come on, come on, this is no sight for children,' and went home, remaining depressed for the rest of the day, snapping at the children unnecessarily. Since that day she had never gone back. She even disliked Sam in his large muddied boots as he clumped about the wood floor of the site hut, a yellow helmet tipped to the back of his head. While she was there Sam had shouted at one old workman, shouted so much that the spit had spun out of his mouth, then when the man had scurried away he turned and talked normally to her and the boys again.

'How *is* Sam?' Father Malachy asked, as if peering into her mind.

'He's fine,' she said. 'He's a hard man to deal with sometimes.'

'Sure, don't I know that from the wedding,' said Father Malachy.

Mary laughed remembering, then said, 'He fairly laid into the church that day.'

' 'Tis sad all the same.'

'But he was only joking,' Mary protested.

'I know, but it's sad anyway. Does he cause you any trouble . . . about your faith?' he asked.

'Ach, no, sure I've . . . we never talk about it.'

Father Malachy persisted. 'He's never shown any desire to join has he?'

'No Father, he's not interested in religion of any breed.'

Father Malachy cracked the stiffening joints of his fingers and stared again at the pelmet.

'Perhaps seeing your good example, he may, someday. You've no idea how it impresses non-believers to see us Catholics getting up out of our beds for early mass every morning.'

'I don't go to mass any more, Father . . . on weekdays.'

'Oh, but you still go on Sundays,' he said smiling.

'Yes Father.'

Father Malachy put the cup to his head and drank all but the tea leaves and set the rattling cup and saucer over on the sideboard.

'Last Sunday's epistle was the boy eh? St Paul could always hit the nail on the head.'

'Indeed Father. There's more tea in the pot,' she said aiming the spout at him like a duelling pistol.

'No, no more for me,' he said writhing in his chair, hunting his pockets for cigarettes. As he did so he made hollow clumping noises with his false teeth prior to smoking. He produced an untipped brand that he had been smoking since his days in the seminary, a brand that Mary had only seen in the

21

Republic on holidays. He lit one and while inhaling picked the specks of tobacco off his tongue with finger and thumb. . 'And there's no more family on the way?' he said suddenly as if continuing from something.

'No Father, why? Should there be?'

'No . . . no,' he said lightly.

'We had the children we wanted. Then Deirdre was a mis . . .. Deirdre was a mistake.'

Father Malachy looked at her, almost smiling, through the triangle formed by his fingers.

'We use the rhythm method, Father, that's allowed by the church isn't it?'

'I'm not prying Mary. I know you well enough and I know the difficulties, especially when you're married to a man who has no . . . well, let's just say he's not in agreement with the Church.'

'What does the Church know about sex anyway. They're in no position to judge.'

'We can be unemotional about it, at least.'

Mary, not wanting to get involved, did not reply and the afternoon progressed made up of great slabs of silence. During the silences she would think of something to do in the kitchen, or when she actually ran out of chores she excused herself and went out, folded her arms, leaned against the sink unit and flashed her eyes to heaven.

At one stage she remembered about the children upstairs and knew they were too quiet. She said this to Father Malachy then opened the door and shouted, 'What are you two doing up there?'

She cocked her head to one side, awaiting the reply. Patricia's voice came clear down the stairs.

'We found Mammy's clock with the tablets in.'

Mary rushed out snapping the door shut behind her. She came back after some minutes, flushed and carrying Deirdre. Patricia's cries from upstairs pierced the air for a long time. Father Malachy smiling from ear to dentured ear said, 'Children can be an awful nuisance at times.'

He leaned forward and tried to tickle Deirdre under the chin, but she girned and put her head under Mary's arm.

'When will this lady be going to the nuns?' he said in a baby voice which didn't suit him.

'She's only two! Don't talk to me about nuns.'

'I don't like them either but they certainly gave *you* a grounding in your faith that'll stand by you. Your mother and father, God rest them, gave them a great foundation to build on. That's why you're strong enough to survive, Mary.'

'I know Father, it's not their religious teaching, but the way they pried that I hated.'

Then she told him how Sister Benedict had found the social position of every girl in the class after one Maths lesson. She gave sums on how long it would take a girl to clean a house of ten fifty square feet at such and such a pace. Hands up how many girls have detached houses, semi-detached houses, terrace houses? How many girls have maids to help with the cleaning? Another sum of distance travelled per gallon of petrol ended in a classification of those girls with or without cars and if they had a car what type it was. Rolls, Jag, Ford, Austin and so on. Sister Benedict was the girl. After this lesson the rows in the class were rearranged.

Father Malachy laughed, his hands up in defence saying, 'Charity, Mary, charity.'

Mary felt a bit spent after her outburst and there followed another period of silence. She was glad that Deirdre was there at her knee, because she could croon over her, making childish conversation to fill the gaps. Then she explained to Father Malachy that the child usually slept for a while in the afternoons. While she was up the stairs putting her into her cot she heard the front door slam. 'Who's that?' she shouted.

It was the boys.

Patricia had gone out to the garden to sulk.

The boys were talking and mumbling in the hallway, again too quiet for Mary's liking. She hung over the banisters and looked down. The two boys were crouched on the carpet, Father Malachy's case open in front of them, exploring. Mary rushed down the stairs, her voice compressed with anger hissing, 'Get out, you nosey brats.'

23

She smacked Rodney hard on the back of his head with her bony hand but John was away before she could draw back and hit him. Rodney ran, his mouth hanging black and open in a cry which had not yet been translated into sound. She slammed the door after them and hunkered down to fix the case. She squatted for what seemed a long time looking into the case, expecting the front door to open at any second. A pair of striped pyjamas, grey and maroon, more old fashioned than her father had worn when he was alive, long cream woollen combinations, a tin of powder for cleaning dentures, a jar of yellow capsules, a handful of holy pictures, only the gold haloes catching the light like a scatter of coins. She lifted the combinations, trying to look underneath without disturbing them. A breviary and a paperback detective. She pulled back the elasticated pocket at the side, saw only an old cigarette, a dry white arc, then she put all the clothes back as she thought they should have been. She was conscious of a throbbing bruise beneath her wedding ring, where she had hit the thick bone of Rodney's skull for doing what she was now doing herself. She closed the case and as quietly as she could snapped the lock shut. Brushing down the folds of her dress, she rose and went in to Father Malachy feeling a slight tremor in her knees as she walked.

After a while he asked her: 'What time does Sam come in at?'

'Oh, you can never tell with Sam.' Then she added, 'I suppose you'll be going up to see Jimmy Brankin as usual, Father.'

It was a long time before he replied.

'Poor Jimmy's dead, God rest him.' Then his mouth turned downwards at the corners, like a fish mouth. His face seemed to crumble and collapse but he rubbed his cheeks hard with the palms of his hands and prevented himself from crying.

'Oh, I didn't know,' said Mary, her mouth remaining in the 'O' position. He seemed not to hear her but went on talking.

'In December. He was stupid too, to be an oul bachelor, when he had the choice. A wife and children take the cold out of the air. But he's away.'

He rubbed his cheeks vigorously again so that his speech was deformed. Mary heard him say something about new friends being hard to make. She became embarrassed and went forward to sweep the hearth. Without looking at him she tried to comfort, saying, 'But you're holy. What about God?'

'Of the spirit, little comfort, little comfort.'

Then he jumped up, surprisingly sprightly, and said, 'I must get to Smithfield before it closes. Belfast would be nothing without a visit to Smithfield.'

He bent backwards to get the stiffness out of his bones, for it was the first time he had been out of the chair since he arrived. Mary followed him into the hall and as he picked up his case, heard the handle squeak. He opened the catch on the door and extended his hand to Mary.

'Goodbye Mary, please God I'll see you next year.'

'But where will you stay, now that Jimmy's . . .'.

'I know a hotel that's good in University Road. My curate has stayed . . .'.

'You'll do no such thing,' said Mary sharply. 'You'll stay here in the spare room.'

He refused and blustered for some time, then quietly let Mary take his case from him.

'But I'll go on down the town anyway. You can tell Sam before I get back. God bless you.'

He turned to go, then remembered something. He sunk his hand deep into his pocket. 'Here, there's a few wee medals I got from Lourdes. You can pin them on the children's vests.' He said it in a tone that belittled the present as he pressed them into her hand.

'Oh you *shouldn't*, you really shouldn't.'

He waved his hand over his shoulder as he walked away. 'The wee bits of religion about the children does them no harm.'

Mary closed the door and sighed to herself, 'Oh Jesus, Sam,' then put the case in the alcove under the stairs. She went to the front room and left the medals, almost too light for metal, on the mantlepiece. She cleared the tea things and washed them. Back in the front room again she stood for a moment at the fireplace, then scraped the medals off the mantlepiece as she had seen Sam draw a pool to him at poker and put them in her handbag where they wouldn't be seen.

25

A Happy Birthday

Sammy adjusted his tie in front of the mirror and tucked in the frayed cuffs of his shirt sleeves. He whistled a few bars of something and whatever way he was holding his mouth he noticed he had missed a few copper-coloured hairs at the angle of his lip. He got out his razor again and dipped in his mug of now luke-warm water. He opened his mouth in a mock yawn and nicked off the remaining hairs. Next he combed his hair, shading it so low at the side of his head that it covered at least half of the bald area. He sang aloud as he did so. His mother spoke out from the kitchen.

'You're in the quare mood to-day.'

Sammy carried his mug out to the kitchen and offered it to his mother, saying, 'Like a nice cup of warm hairs, Ma?'

She made a face, calling him a dirty baste as he threw them down the sink.

'Why shouldn't I be in the quare mood?' said Sammy. 'Fifty to-day and they're paying out on the dole too.' His mother wiped her hands nervously on her apron.

'Don't be drinking, son, sure you won't?' Sammy said he wouldn't.

'Promise me,' she said and he nodded, while making another attempt to spread the hairs more evenly over the skin of his head at the mirror in the kitchen.

'Have you any bus fare Ma?'

'What's wrong with your legs?' she asked. Sammy stooped very low trying to see the sky above the backyard wall.

'Looks a bit like rain,' he said. His mother shuffled into

the room.

'Where's my purse?' she said, stooping into the corner for her bag. 'Do you think I'm made of money, eh? The pension doesn't go too far when you're around.' Sammy slipped the two bob into his pocket and said he would pay her back when he got his money.

'I've heard that before,' said his mother. Sammy left the house and walked slowly into town.

On his way down the road he called into Forsythes and bought four cigarettes. The girl rolled them across the counter to him and he examined them, checking the brand. He asked for a packet and the girl sorted one out from beneath the counter, and slipped the cigarettes into it. Sammy patted them happily in his pocket. On the street he asked a man for a light and inhaled deeply the first of the day. He reached the town half an hour before he had to sign on so he went into the library to read the newspapers. Nothing but bloody explosions and robberies again. Something would have to be done. The IRA was getting the run of the country without one to say boo to them. *Something* would have to be done. He made his way to the bureau at about five to eleven. It was the cheeky wee bitch who was paying out. When he got his money he peeled off two pounds for his mother and stuck them in his top pocket out of the way. Then he headed for the pub where he knew all the boys would be.

When Sammy came out the bright sunlight was a great shock to him. As he walked along the street the walls seemed to come at him and nudge him. People deliberately went out of their way to veer into his path. The bus driver smiled at him for no reason and some young ones clapped after he had sung a song. He got off the bus and walked past a line of soldiers at the main gate. He stopped with the last one and put his hand on his arm and said,

'Yis are doing a grand job.'

'Wot?' said the soldier.

'Yis are the boys.' The soldier's gun as he leaned over to try and hear pointed to the middle of Sammy's chest.

'Wot?' he said.

'Forget it,' said Sammy. He moved off through the gates towards the exhibition hall. A group of student demonstrators paraded silently weaving their way in and out of the domes. They carried placards — 'ULSTER 71 WHITEWASH', 'EXPOSE 71'. Sammy made his way in front of one with long hair and stopped him with his hand. He held him at arm's length, focusing the writing on the card. 'TELL THE TRUTH, 40,000 UNEMPLOYED'. Sammy leaned closer to him.

'Why don't yis catch yourselves on?' The student began to move forward. 'Who do you think is paying your grants for you, eh? You'll get no work coming to the country with the likes of you parading about making trouble.' The first student had pushed past him but he continued speaking to the next in line.

'Yis have never done a day's work in your lives. You don't know what ye're talking about. So-called civil rights. Why don't yis go down south where yis belong?' A policeman came up behind him and guided him away. Sammy went past the exhibition hall and found the blue igloo of the bar tent. He fingered into his top pocket and pulled out the two pounds. He had more stout, he didn't know how many, and now that he was in his own company he had a whiskey with each one. After a time he heard squealing coming from outside the tent and went out to see what it was about.

A crowd of girls were on the Hurricane Waltzer. Sammy talked to the man operating it until the session finished, then he paid his money and climbed up into a seat, being guided by hands from behind. The attendant locked him in with a bar. Sammy called to the girls who were paying their money for another turn, but the words came out all wrong. The machine started, clanking and grinding, spinning slowly. It gathered speed and began to loop and dip. The noise of the Waltzer was reaching a crescendo but at each sudden drop the squealing of the girls rose above it. Sammy's hand tightened convulsively on the bar in front of him. He saw the upturned watching faces streak into one and other. Then he opened his mouth and it all came out.

Below people screamed and ran, covering their heads. One

woman quickly put up her umbrella. The student demonstrators sheltered beneath their placards. It came out of him like sparks from a catherine wheel. An emulsion of minestrone-stout. Spraying on the multi-coloured domes of the exhibition. Exclamation marks, yellow and buff bird-dung streaks flecking the çanvas. Sparking off the tarmac paths, soaking spots in people's Sunday best. Children slipped and fell. The machine operator and his mate stayed in their hut throughout. People signalled frantically, pointing to the revolving figure.

When the Waltzer came to a halt Sammy's mouth was still open. As the operator was unlocking the safety bar Sammy belched and the operator dived to one side. As Sammy staggered away, the operator said to his mate, 'There's not a spot of boke on him.'

And he replied, 'He's probably the only one in the park.'

Sammy walked in a great arc and arrived back to the operator. His flap of hair hung by his ear and his head shone. 'What's there to see here?' he asked. His elbow slipped off the edge of the counter and he belched loudly again.

The operator pointed. 'Do you see that wee girl over there?' Sammy looked at the pointing finger but not at its direction. 'She'll tell you all you want to know.'

He turned Sammy by the shoulders and aimed him in the direction of the information kiosk. When he asked the same question the girl with the skill of a thousand rehearsals told him all there was to see. Sammy swayed looking at her, blinking, then he looked down at his toes. His fingers fished for his last pound.

'Thanks,' he said. 'I'll maybe go for a drink first. It's my birthday.'

Secrets

He had been called to be there at the end. His Great Aunt Mary had been dying for some days now and the house was full of relatives. He had just left his girlfriend home — they had been studying for 'A' levels together — and had come back to the house to find all the lights spilling onto the lawn and a sense of purpose which had been absent from the last few days.

He knelt at the bedroom door to join in the prayers. His knees were on the wooden threshold and he edged them forward onto the carpet. They had tried to wrap her fingers around a crucifix but they kept loosening. She lay low on the pillow and her face seemed to have shrunk by half since he had gone out earlier in the night. Her white hair was damped and pushed back from her forehead. She twisted her head from side to side, her eyes closed. The prayers chorused on, trying to cover the sound she was making deep in her throat. Someone said about her teeth and his mother leaned over her and said, 'That's the pet', and took her dentures from her mouth. The lower half of her face seemed to collapse. She half opened her eyes but could not raise her eyelids enough and showed only crescents of white.

'Hail Mary full of grace . . .' the prayers went on. He closed his hands over his face so that he would not have to look but smelt the trace of his girlfriend's handcream from his hands. The noise, deep and guttural, that his aunt was making became intolerable to him. It was as if she were drowning. She had lost all the dignity he knew her to have. He got up from the floor and stepped between the others who were kneeling and went into her sitting-room off the same landing.

He was trembling with anger or sorrow, he didn't know which. He sat in the brightness of her big sitting-room at the oval table and waited for something to happen. On the table was a cut-glass vase of irises, dying because she had been in bed for over a week. He sat staring at them. They were withering from the tips inward, scrolling themselves delicately, brown and neat. Clearing up after themselves. He stared at them for a long time until he heard the sounds of women weeping from the next room.

*   *   *

His aunt had been small — her head on a level with his when she sat at her table — and she seemed to get smaller each year. Her skin fresh, her hair white and waved and always well washed. She wore no jewelry except a cameo ring on the third finger of her right hand and, around her neck, a gold locket on a chain. The white classical profile on the ring was almost worn through and had become translucent and indistinct. The boy had noticed the ring when she had read to him as a child. In the beginning fairy tales, then as he got older extracts from famous novels, *Lorna Doone, Persuasion, Wuthering Heights* and her favourite extract, because she read it so often, Pip's meeting with Miss Havisham from *Great Expectations*. She would sit with him on her knee, her arms around him and holding the page flat with her hand. When he was bored he would interrupt her and ask about the ring. He loved hearing her tell of how her grandmother had given it to her as a brooch and she had had a ring made from it. He would try to count back to see how old it was. Had her grandmother got it from *her* grandmother? And if so what had she turned it into? She would nod her head from side to side and say, 'How would I know a thing like that?' keeping her place in the closed book with her finger.

'Don't be so inquisitive,' she'd say. 'Let's see what happens next in the story.'

One day she was sitting copying figures into a long narrow book with a dip pen when he came into her room. She didn't look up but when he asked her a question she just said, 'Mm?' and went on writing. The vase of irises on the oval table vibrated slightly as she wrote.

'What is it?' She wiped the nib on blotting paper and looked up at him over her reading glasses.

'I've started collecting stamps and Mamma says you might have some.'

'Does she now —?'

She got up from the table and went to the tall walnut bureau-bookcase standing in the alcove. From a shelf of the bookcase she took a small wallet of keys and selected one for the lock. There was a harsh metal shearing sound as she pulled the desk flap down. The writing area was covered with green leather which had dog-eared at the corners. The inner part was divided into pigeon holes, all bulging with papers. Some of them, envelopes, were gathered in batches nipped at the waist with elastic bands. There were postcards and bills and cash-books. She pointed to the postcards.

'You may have the stamps on those,' she said. 'But don't tear them. Steam them off.'

She went back to the oval table and continued writing. He sat on the arm of the chair looking through the picture post-cards — torchlight processions at Lourdes, brown photographs of town centres, dull black and whites of beaches backed by faded hotels. Then he turned them over and began to sort the stamps. Spanish, with a bald man, French with a rooster, German with funny jerky print, some Italian with what looked like a chimney-sweep's bundle and a hatchet.

'These are great,' he said. 'I haven't got any of them.'

'Just be careful how you take them off.'

'Can I take them downstairs?'

'Is your mother there?'

'Yes.'

'Then perhaps it's best if you bring the kettle up here.'

He went down to the kitchen. His mother was in the morning room polishing silver. He took the kettle and the flex upstairs. Except for the dipping and scratching of his Aunt's pen the room was silent. It was at the back of the house overlooking the orchard and the sound of traffic from the main road was distant and muted. A tiny rattle began as the kettle warmed up, then it bubbled and steam gushed quietly from its spout. The cards began to curl slightly in the jet of steam but she didn't seem to be watching. The stamps peeled moistly off and he put them in a saucer of water to flatten them.

'Who is Brother Benignus?' he asked. She seemed not to hear. He asked again and she looked over her glasses.

'He was a friend.'

His flourishing signature appeared again and again. Sometimes Bro Benignus, sometimes Benignus and once Iggy.

'Is he alive?'

'No, he's dead now. Watch the kettle doesn't run dry.'

When he had all the stamps off he put the postcards together and replaced them in the pigeon-hole. He reached over towards the letters but before his hand touched them his aunt's voice, harsh for once, warned.

'A-A-A,' she moved her pen from side to side.' Do-not-touch,' she said and smiled. 'Anything else, yes! That section, no!' She resumed her writing.

The boy went through some other papers and found some photographs. One was of a beautiful girl. It was very old-fashioned but he could see that she was beautiful. The picture was a pale brown oval set on a white square of card. The edges of the oval were misty. The girl in the photograph was young and had dark, dark hair scraped severely back and tied like a knotted rope on the top of her head — high arched eyebrows, her nose straight and thin, her mouth slightly smiling, yet not smiling — the way a mouth is after smiling. Her eyes looked out at him dark and knowing and beautiful.

'Who is that?' he asked.

'Why? What do you think of her?'

'She's all right.'

'Do you think she is beautiful?' The boy nodded.

'That's me,' she said. The boy was glad he had pleased her in return for the stamps.

Other photographs were there, not posed ones like Aunt Mary's but Brownie snaps of laughing groups of girls in bucket hats like German helmets and coats to their ankles. They seemed tiny faces covered in clothes. There was a photograph of a young man smoking a cigarette, his hair combed one way by the wind against a background of sea.

'Who is that in the uniform?' the boy asked.

'He's a soldier,' she answered without looking up.

'Oh,' said the boy. 'But who is he?'

'He was a friend of mine before you were born,' she said Then added, 'Do I smell something cooking? Take your stamps and off you go. That's the boy.'

The boy looked at the back of the picture of the man and saw in black spidery ink 'John, Aug '15 Ballintoye'.

'I thought maybe it was Brother Benignus,' he said. She looked at him not answering.

'Was your friend killed in the war?'

At first she said no, but then she changed her mind.

'Perhaps he was,' she said, then smiled. 'You are far too inquisitive. Put it to use and go and see what is for tea. Your mother will need the kettle.' She came over to the bureau and helped tidy the photographs away. Then she locked it and put the keys on the shelf.

'Will you bring me up my tray?'

The boy nodded and left.

*   *   *

It was a Sunday evening, bright and summery. He was doing his homework and his mother was sitting on the carpet in one of her periodic fits of tidying out the drawers of the mahogany sideboard. On one side of her was a heap of paper scraps torn in quarters and bits of rubbish, on the other the useful items that had to be kept. The boy heard the bottom stair creak under Aunt Mary's light footstep. She knocked and put her head round the door and said that she was walking to Devotions. She was dressed in her good coat and hat and was just easing her fingers into her second glove. The boy saw her stop and pat her hair into place before the mirror in the hallway. His mother stretched over and slammed the door shut. It vibrated, then he heard the deeper sound of the outside door

34

closing and her first few steps on the gravelled driveway. He sat for a long time wondering if he would have time or not. Devotions could take anything from twenty minutes to three quarters of an hour, depending on who was saying it.

Ten minutes must have passed, then the boy left his homework and went upstairs and into his aunt's sitting room. He stood in front of the bureau wondering, then he reached for the keys. He tried several before he got the right one. The desk flap screeched as he pulled it down. He pretended to look at the postcards again in case there were any stamps he had missed. Then he put them away and reached for the bundle of letters. The elastic band was thick and old, brittle almost and when he took it off its track remained on the wad of letters. He carefully opened one and took out the letter and unfolded it, frail, khaki-coloured.

> My dearest Mary, it began. I am so tired I can hardly write to you. I have spent what seems like all day censoring letters (there is a howitzer about 100 yds away firing every 2 minutes). The letters are heartrending in their attempt to express what they cannot. Some of the men are illiterate, others almost so. I know that they feel as much as we do, yet they do not have the words to express it. That is your job in the schoolroom to give us generations who can read and write well. They have . . .

The boy's eye skipped down the page and over the next. He read the last paragraph.

> Mary I love you as much as ever — more so that we cannot be together. I do not know which is worse, the hurt of this war or being separated from you. Give all my love to Brendan and all at home.

It was signed, scribbled with what he took to be John. He folded the paper carefully into its original creases and put it in the envelope. He opened another.

My love, it is thinking of you that keeps me sane. When I get a moment I open my memories of you as if I were reading. Your long dark hair — I always imagine you wearing the blouse with the tiny roses, the white one that opened down the back — your eyes that said so much without words, the way you lowered your head when I said anything that embarrassed you, and the clean nape of your neck.

The day I think about most was the day we climbed the head at Ballycastle. In a hollow, out of the wind, the air full of pollen and the sound of insects, the grass warm and dry and you lying beside me your hair undone, between me and the sun. You remember that that was where I first kissed you and the look of disbelief in your eyes that made me laugh afterwards.

It makes me laugh now to see myself savouring these memories standing alone up to my thighs in muck. It is everywhere, two, three feet deep. To walk ten yards leaves you quite breathless.

I haven't time to write more today so I leave you with my feet in the clay and my head in the clouds. I love you, John.

He did not bother to put the letter back into the envelope but opened another.

My dearest, I am so cold that I find it difficult to keep my hand steady enough to write. You remember when we swam the last two fingers of your hand went the colour and texture of candles with the cold. Well that is how I am all over. It is almost four days since I had any real sensation in my feet or legs. Everything is frozen. The ground is like steel.

Forgive me telling you this but I feel I have to say it to someone. The worst thing is the dead. They sit or lie frozen in the position they died. You can distinguish them from the living because their faces

36

are the colour of slate. God help us when the thaw comes . . . This war is beginning to have an effect on me. I have lost all sense of feeling. The only emotion I have experienced lately is one of anger. Sheer white trembling anger. I have no pity or sorrow for the dead and injured. I thank God it is not me but I am enraged that it had to be them. If I live through this experience I will be a different person.

The only thing that remains constant is my love for you.

Today a man died beside me. A piece of shrapnel had pierced his neck as we were moving under fire. I pulled him into a crater and stayed with him until he died. I watched him choke and then drown in his blood.

I am full of anger which has no direction.

He sorted through the pile and read half of some, all of others. The sun had fallen low in the sky and shone directly into the room onto the pages he was reading making the paper glare. He selected a letter from the back of the pile and shaded it with his hand as he read.

Dearest Mary, I am writing this to you from my hospital bed. I hope that you were not too worried about not hearing from me. I have been here, so they tell me, for two weeks and it took another two weeks before I could bring myself to write this letter.

I have been thinking a lot as I lie here about the war and about myself and about you. I do not know how to say this but I feel deeply that I must do something, must sacrifice something to make up for the horror of the past year. In some strange way Christ has spoken to me through the carnage . . .

Suddenly the boy heard the creak of the stair and he frantically tried to slip the letter back into its envelope but it crumpled and would not fit. He bundled them all together. He could hear his aunt's familiar puffing on the short stairs to her room. He spread the elastic band wide with his fingers. It snapped and the letters scattered. He pushed them into their pigeon hole and quickly closed the desk flap. The brass screeched loudly and clicked shut. At that moment his aunt came into the room.

'What are you doing boy?' she snapped.

'Nothing.' He stood with the keys in his hand. She walked to the bureau and opened it. The letters sprung out in an untidy heap.

'You have been reading my letters,' she said quietly. Her mouth was tight with the words and her eyes blazed. The boy could say nothing. She struck him across the side of the face.

'Get out,' she said. 'Get out of my room.'

The boy, the side of his face stinging and red, put the keys on the table on his way out. When he reached the door she called to him. He stopped, his hand on the handle.

'You are dirt,' she hissed, 'and always will be dirt. I shall remember this till the day I die.'

*   *   *

Even though it was a warm evening there was a fire in the large fireplace. His mother had asked him to light it so that she could clear out Aunt Mary's stuff. The room could then be his study, she said. She came in and seeing him at the table said, 'I hope I'm not disturbing you.'

'No.'

She took the keys from her pocket, opened the bureau and began burning papers and cards. She glanced quickly at each one before she flicked it onto the fire.

'Who was Brother Benignus?' he asked.

His mother stopped sorting and said, 'I don't know. Your aunt kept herself very much to herself. She got books from him through the post occasionally. That much I do know.'

She went on burning the cards. They built into strata, glowing red and black. Now and again she broke up the pile with the poker, sending showers of sparks up the chimney. He saw her come to the letters. She took off the elastic band and put it to one side with the useful things and began dealing the envelopes into the fire. She opened one and read quickly through it, then threw it on top of the burning pile.

'Mama,' he said.

'Yes?'

'Did Aunt Mary say anything about me?'

'What do you mean?'

'Before she died — did she say anything?'

'Not that I know of — the poor thing was too far gone to speak, God rest her.' She went on burning, lifting the corners of the letters with the poker to let the flames underneath them.

When he felt a hardness in his throat he put his head down on his books. Tears came into his eyes for the first time since she had died and he cried silently into the crook of his arm for the woman who had been his maiden aunt, his teller of tales, that she might forgive him.

The Miraculous Candidate

At the age of fourteen John began to worry about the effects of his sanctity. The first thing had been a tingling, painful sensation in the palms of his hands and the soles of his feet. But an even more alarming symptom was the night when, as he fervently prayed himself to sleep, he felt himself being lifted up a full foot and a half above the bed — bedclothes and all. The next morning when he thought about it he dismissed it as a dream or the result of examination nerves.

Now on the morning of his Science exam he felt his stomach light and woolly, as if he had eaten feathers for breakfast. Outside the gym some of the boys fenced with new yellow rulers or sat drumming them on their knees. The elder ones, doing Senior and 'A' levels, stood in groups all looking very pale, one turning now and again to spit over his shoulder to show he didn't care. John checked for his examination card which his grandmother had carefully put in his inside pocket the night before. She had also pinned a Holy Ghost medal beneath his lapel where it wouldn't be seen and made him wear his blazer while she brushed it. She had asked him what Science was about and when John tried to explain she had interrupted him saying, 'If y'can blether as well with your pen — you'll do all right.'

One of the Seniors said it was nearly half-past and they all began to shuffle towards the door of the gym. John had been promised a watch if he passed his Junior.

The doors were opened and they all filed quietly to their places. John's desk was at the back with his number chalked on the top right-hand corner. He sat down, unclipped his fountain-pen and set it in the groove. All the desks had an empty hole for an ink-well. During the Maths exam one of the boys opposite who couldn't do any of the questions drew a face in biro on his finger and put it up through the hole and waggled it at John. He didn't seem to care whether he failed or not.

John sat looking at the wall-bars which lined the gym. The invigilator held up a brown paper parcel and pointed to the unbroken seal, then opened it, tearing off the paper noisily. He had a bad foot and some sort of high boot which squeaked every time he took a step. His face was pale and full of suspicion. He was always jumping up suddenly as if he had caught somebody on, flicking back his stringy hair as he did so. When he ate the tea and biscuits left at the door for him at eleven his eyes kept darting back and forward. John noticed that he 'gullied', a term his grandmother used for chewing and drinking tea at the same time. When reading, he never held the newspaper up but laid it flat on the table and stood propped on his arms, his big boot balanced on its toe to take the weight off it.

'If you ever meet the devil you'll know him by his cloven hoof,' his Granny had told him. A very holy woman, she had made it her business to read to him every Sunday night from the lives of the Saints, making him sit at her feet as she did so. While she read she let her glasses slip down to the end of her long nose and would look over them every so often, to see if he was listening. She had a mole on her chin with a hair like a watch-spring growing out of it. She read in a serious voice, very different to her ordinary one, and always blew on the fine tissuey pages to separate them before turning over with her trembling fingers. She had great faith and had a particular saint for every difficulty. 'St Blaise is good for throats and if you've ever lost anything St Anthony'll find it for you.' She always kept a sixpence under the statue of the Child of Prague because then, she said, she'd never be without. Above all there was St Joseph of Cupertino. For examinations he was your man. Often she read his bit out of the book to John.

'Don't sit with your back to the fire or you'll melt the marrow of your bones,' and he'd change his position at her feet and listen intently.

St Joseph was so close to God that sometimes when he prayed he was lifted up off the ground. Other times when he'd be carrying plates — he was only smart enough to work in the kitchen — he would go into a holy trance and break every dish on the tiled floor. He wanted to become a priest but he was very stupid so he learned off just one line of the Bible. But here — and this was the best part of the story — when his exam came didn't God make the Bishop ask him the one line he knew and he came through with flying colours. When the story was finished his Granny always said, 'It was all he was fit for, God help him — the one line.'

The ingivilator squeaked his way down towards John and flicked a pink exam paper onto his desk. John steadied it with his hand. His eyes raced across the lines looking for the familiar questions. The feathers whirlpooled almost into his throat. He panicked. There was not a single question — *not one* — he knew anything about. He tried to settle himself and concentrated to read the first question.

> State Newton's Universal Law of Gravitation. Give arguments for or against the statement that 'the only reason an apple falls downwards to meet the earth instead of the earth falling upwards to meet the apple is that the earth, being much more massive exerts the greater pull.' The mass of the moon is one eighty-first, and its radius one quarter that of the earth. What is the acceleration of gravity at its surface if . . .

It was no use. He couldn't figure out what was wrong. He had been to mass and communion every day for the past year — he had prayed hard for the right questions. The whole family had prayed hard for the right questions. What sort of return was this? He suppressed the thought because it was . . . it was God's will. Perhaps a watch would lead him into sin somehow or other?

He looked round at the rest of the boys. Most of them were writing frantically. Others sat sucking their pens or doodling on their rough-work sheets. John looked at the big clock they had hung on the wall-bars with its second hand slowly spinning. Twenty minutes had gone already and he hadn't put pen to paper. He must do *something*.

He closed his eyes very tight and clenching his fists to the side of his head he placed himself in God's hands and began to pray. His Granny's voice came to him. 'The Patron Saint of Examinations. Pray to him if you're really stuck'. He saw the shining damp of his palms, then pressed them to his face. Now he summoned up his whole being, focused it to a point of white heat. All the good that he had ever done, that he ever would do, all his prayers, the sum total of himself, he concentrated into the name of the Saint. He clenched his eyes so hard there was a roaring in his ears. His finger-nails bit into his cheeks. His lips moved and he said, 'Saint Joseph of Cupertino, help me.'

He opened his eyes and saw that somehow he was above his desk. Not far — he was raised up about a foot and a half, his body still in a sitting position. The invigilator looked up from his paper and John tried to lower himself back down into his seat. But he had no control over his limbs. The invigilator came round his desk quickly and walked towards him over the coconut matting, his boot creaking as he came.

'What are you up to?' he hissed between his teeth.

'Nothing,' whispered John. He could feel his cheeks becoming more and more red, until his whole face throbbed with blushing.

'Are you trying to copy?' The invigilator's face was on a level with the boy's. 'You can see every word the boy in front of you is writing, can't you?'

'No sir, I'm not trying to . . .' stammered John. 'I was just praying and . . .' The man looked like a Protestant. The Ministry brought in teachers from other schools. Protestant schools. He wouldn't understand about Saints.

'I don't care what you say you were doing. I think you are trying to copy and if you don't come down from there I'll have you disqualified.' The little man was getting as red in the face as John.

'I can't sir.'

'Very well then.' The invigilator clicked his tongue angrily and walked creak-padding away to his desk.

John again concentrated his whole being, focused it to a prayer of white heat.

'Saint Joseph of Cupertino. *Get me down please.*' But nothing happened. The invigilator lifted his clip-board with the candidates' names and started back towards John. Some of the boys in the back row had stopped writing and were laughing. The invigilator reached him.

'Are you going to come down from there or not?'

'I can't.' The tears welled up in John's eyes.

'Then I shall have to ask you to leave.'

'I can't,' said John.

The invigilator leaned forward and tapped the boy in front of John on the shoulder.

'Do you mind for a moment?' he said and turned the boy's answer paper face downwards on the desk. While he was turned away John frantically tried to think of a way out. His prayer hadn't worked....maybe a sin would . . . the invigilator turned to him.

'For the last time I'm . . .'

'Fuck the Pope,' said John and as he did so, he plumped back down into his seat skinning his shin on the tubular frame of the desk.

'Pardon. What did you say?' asked the invigilator.

'Nothing sir. It's all right now. I'm sorry sir.'

'What *is* wrong with you boy?'

'I can't do it, sir — any of it.' John pointed to the paper. The invigilator spun it round with his finger.

'You should have thought of that some months ago . . .' The words faded away. 'I'm very sorry. Just a minute,' he said, limping very quickly down to his desk. He came back with a white exam paper which he put in front of John.

'Very sorry,' he repeated. 'It does happen sometimes.'

John looked for the first time at the head of the pink paper.

ADVANCED LEVEL PHYSICS. Now he read quickly through the questions on the white paper the invigilator had brought him. They were all there. Archimedes in his bath, properties of NaC1, allotropes of sulphur, the anatomy of the buttercup. The invigilator smiled with his spade-like teeth.

'Is that any better?' he asked. John nodded. '. . . and if you need some extra time to make up, you can have it.'

'Thank you sir,' said John. The invigilator hunkered down beside him and whispered confidentially.

'This wee mix-up'll not go any farther than between ourselves, will it . . .' He looked down at his clip-board. '. . .Johnny?'

'No sir.'

He gave John a pat on the back and creaked away over the coconut matting. John put his head down on the desk and uttered a prayer of Thanksgiving to St Joseph of Cupertino, this time making sure to keep his fervour within bounds.

Between Two Shores

It was dark and he sat with his knees tucked up to his chin, knowing there was a long night ahead of him. He had arrived early for the boat and sat alone in a row of seats wishing he had bought a paper or a magazine of some sort. He heard a noise like a pulse from somewhere deep in the boat. Later he changed his position and put his feet on the floor.

For something to do he opened his case and looked again at the presents he had for the children. A painting by numbers set for the eldest boy of the 'Laughing Cavalier', for the three girls, dolls, horizontal with their eyes closed, a blonde, a red-head and a brunette to prevent fighting over who owned which. He had also bought a trick pack of cards. He bought these for himself but he didn't like to admit it. He saw himself amazing his incredulous, laughing father after dinner by turning the whole pack into the seven of clubs or whatever else he liked by just tapping them as the man in the shop had done.

The trick cards would be a nice way to start a conversation if anybody sat down beside him, so he put them on top of his clothes in the case. He locked it and slipped it off the seat, leaving it vacant. Other people were beginning to come into the lounge lugging heavy cases. When they saw him sitting in the middle of the row they moved on to find another. He found their Irish accents grating and flat.

He lit a cigarette and as he put the matches back in his pocket his fingers closed around his wife's present. He took it out, a small jeweller's box, black with a domed top. As he clicked back the lid he saw again the gold against the red satin and thought it beautiful. A locket was something permanent, something she could keep for ever. Suddenly his stomach reeled at the thought. He tried to put it out of his mind, snapping the box shut and putting it in his breast pocket. He got up and was about to go to the bar when he saw how the place was filling up. It was Thursday and the Easter rush had started. He would sit his ground until the boat moved out. If he kept his seat and got a few pints inside him he might sleep. It would be a long night.

A middle-aged couple moved into the row — they sounded like they were from Belfast. Later an old couple with a mongol girl sat almost opposite him. The girl was like all mongols. It was difficult to tell her age — anywhere between twenty and thirty. He thought of moving away to another seat to be away from the moist, open mouth and the beak nose but it might have hurt the grey haired parents. It would be too obvious, so he nodded a smile and just sat on.

The note of the throbbing engine changed and the lights on the docks began to move slowly past. He had a free seat in front of him and he tried to put his feet up but it was just out of reach. The parents took their mongol daughter 'to see the big ship going out' and he then felt free to move. He found the act of walking strange on the moving ship.

He went to the bar and bought a pint of stout and took it out onto the deck. Every time he travelled he was amazed at the way they edged the huge boat out of the narrow channel — a foot to spare on each side. Then the long wait at the lock gates. Inside, the water flat, roughed only by the wind — out there the waves leaping and chopping, black and slate grey in the light of the moon. Eventually they were away, the boat swinging out to sea and the wind rising, cuffing him on the side of the head. It was cold now and he turned to go in. On a small bench on the open deck he saw a bloke laying out his sleeping bag and sliding down inside it.

He had several more pints in the bar sitting on his own, moving his glass round the four metal indentations. There were men and boys with short hair, obviously British soldiers.

He thought how sick they must be having to go back to Ireland at Easter. There was a nice looking girl sitting alone reading with a rucksack at her feet. She looked like a student. He wondered how he could start to talk to her. His trick cards were in the case and he had nothing with him. She seemed very interested in her book because she didn't even lift her eyes from it as she sipped her beer. She was nice looking, dark hair tied back, large dark eyes following the lines back and forth on the page. He looked at her body, then felt himself recoil as if someone had clanged a handbell in his ear and shouted 'unclean'. Talk was what he wanted. Talk stopped him thinking. When he was alone he felt frightened and unsure. He blamed his trouble on this.

In the beginning London had been a terrible place. During the day he had worked himself to the point of exhaustion. Back at the digs he would wash and shave and after a meal he would drag himself to the pub with the other Irish boys rather than sit at home. He drank at half the pace the others did and would have full pints on the table in front of him when closing time came. Invariably somebody else would drain them, rather than let them go to waste. Everyone but himself was drunk and they would roar home, some of them being sick on the way against a gable wall or up an entry. Some nights, rather than endure this, he sat in his bedroom even though the landlady had said he could come down and watch TV. But it would have meant having to sit with her English husband and their horrible son. Nights like these many times he thought his watch had stopped and he wished he had gone out.

Then one night he'd been taken by ambulance from the digs after vomiting all day with a pain in his gut. When he wakened they had removed his appendix. The man in the next bed was small, dark-haired, friendly. The rest of the ward had nicknamed him 'Mephisto' because of the hours he spent trying to do the crossword in *The Times*. He had never yet completed it. His attention had first been drawn to Nurse Mitchell's legs by this little man who enthused about the shortness of her skirt, the black stockings with the seams, clenching and unclenching his fist. The little man's mind wandered higher and he rolled his small eyes in delight.

In the following days in hospital he fell in love with this Nurse Helen Mitchell. When he asked her about the funny way she talked she said she was from New Zealand. He thought she gave him special treatment. She nursed him back to health, letting him put his arm around when he got out of bed for the first time. He smelt her perfume and felt her firmness. He was astonished at how small she was, having only looked up at her until this. She fitted the crook of his arm like a crutch. Before he left he bought her a present from the hospital shop, of the biggest box of chocolates that they had in stock. Each time she came to his bed it was on the tip of his tongue to ask her out but he didn't have the courage. He had skirted round the question as she made the bed, asking her what she did when she was off duty. She had mentioned the name of a place where she and her friends went for a drink and sometimes a meal.

He had gone home to Donegal for a fortnight at Christmas to recover but on his first night back in London he went to this place and sat drinking alone. On the third night she came in with two other girls. The sight of her out of uniform made him ache to touch her. They sat in the corner not seeing him sitting at the bar. After a couple of whiskeys he went over to them. She looked up, startled almost. He started by saying, 'Maybe you don't remember me . . .'

'Yes, yes I do,' she said laying her hand on his arm. Her two friends smiled at him then went on talking to each other. He said that he just happened to be in that district and remembered the name of the place and thought that he would have liked to see her again. She said yes, that he was the man who bought the *huge* box of chocolates. Her two friends laughed behind their hands. He bought them all a drink. And then insisted again. She said, 'look I'm sorry I've forgotten your name,' and he told her and she introduced him to the others. When time was called he isolated her from the others and asked her if she would like to go out for a meal some night and she said she'd love to.

On the Tuesday after careful shaving and dressing he took her out and afterwards they went back to the flat she shared with the others. He was randy helping her on with her coat at the restaurant, smelling again her perfume, but he intended to play his cards with care and not rush things. But there was no need, because she refused no move he made and her hand was sliding down past his scar before he knew where he was. He was not in control of either himself or her. She changed as he touched her. She bit his tongue and hurt his body with her nails. Dealing with the pain she caused him saved him from coming too soon and disgracing himself.

Afterwards he told her that he was married and she said that she knew but that it made no difference. They both needed something. He asked her if she had done it with many men.

'Many, many men,' she had replied, her New Zealand vowels thin and hard like knives. Tracks of elastic banded her body where her underwear had been. He felt sour and empty and wanted to go back to his digs. She dressed and he liked her better, then she made tea and they were talking again.

Through the next months he saw her many times and they always ended up on the rug before the electric fire and each time his seed left him he thought the loss permanent and irreplaceable.

This girl across the bar reminded him of her, the way she was absorbed in her reading. His nurse, he always called her that, had tried to force him to read books but he had never read a whole book in his life. He had started several for her but he couldn't finish them. He told lies to please her until one day she asked him what he thought of the ending of one she had given him. He felt embarrassed and childish about being found out.

There were some young girls, hardly more than children, drinking at the table across the bar from the soldiers. They were eyeing them and giggling into their vodkas. They had thick Belfast accents. The soldiers wanted nothing to do with them. Soldiers before them had chased it and ended up dead or maimed for life.

An old man had got himself a padded alcove and was in the

process of kicking off his shoes and putting his feet up on his case. There was a hole in the toe of his sock and he crossed his other foot over it to hide it. He remembered an old man telling him on his first trip always to take his shoes off when he slept. Your feet swell when you sleep, he had explained.

The first time leaving had been the worst. He felt somehow it was for good, even though he knew he would be home in two or three months. He had been up since dark getting ready. His wife was frying him bacon and eggs, tip-toeing back and forth putting the things on the table, trying not to wake the children too early. He came up behind her and put his arms round her waist, then moved his hands up to her breasts. She leaned her head back against his shoulder and he saw that she was crying, biting her lip to stop. He knew she would do this, cry in private but she would hold back in front of the others when the mini-bus came.

'Don't,' she said. 'I hear Daddy up.'

That first time the children had to be wakened to see their father off. They appeared outside the house tousleheaded and confused. A mini-bus full of people had pulled into their yard and their Granny and Granda were crying. Handshaking and endless hugging watched by his wife, chalk pale, her forearms folded against the early morning cold. He kissed her once. The people in the mini-bus didn't like to watch. His case went on the pyramid of other cases and the mini-bus bumped over the yard away from the figures grouped around the doorway.

The stout had gone through him and he got up to go to the lavatory. The slight swaying of the boat made it difficult to walk but it was not so bad that he had to use the handles above the urinals. Someone had been sick on the floor, Guinness sick. He looked at his slack flesh held between his fingers at the place where the sore had been. It had all but disappeared. Then a week ago his nurse had noticed it. He had thought nothing of it because it was not painful. She asked him who else he had been sleeping with — insulting him. He had sworn he had been with no one. She explained to him how they were like minute corkscrews going through the whole body. Then she admitted that it must have been her who had picked it up from someone else.

'If not me, then who?' he had asked.

'Never you mind,' she replied. 'My life is my own.'

It was the first time he had seen her concerned. She came after him as he ran down the stairs and implored him to go to a clinic, if not with her, then on his own. But the thought of it terrified him. He had listened to stories on the site of rods being inserted, burning needles and worst of all a thing which opened inside like an umbrella and was forcibly dragged out again. On Wednesday the landlady had said someone had called at the digs looking for him and said he would call back. But he made sure he was out that night and this morning he was up and away early buying presents before getting on the train.

He zipped up his fly and stood looking at himself in the mirror. He looked tired — the long train journey, the sandwiches, smoking too many cigarettes to pass the time. A coppery growth was beginning on his chin. He remembered her biting his tongue, the tearing of her nails, the way she changed. He had not seen her since.

Only once or twice had his wife been like that — changing that way. He knew she would be like that tomorrow night. It was always the same the first night home. But afterwards he knew that it was her, his wife. Even though it was taut with lovemaking her face had something of her care for his children, of the girl and woman, of the kitchen, of dances, of their walks together. He knew who she was as they devoured each other on the creaking bed. In the Bible they knew each other.

Again his mind shied away from the thought. He went out onto the deck to get the smell of sick from about him. Beyond the rail it was black night. He looked down and could see the white bow wave crashing away off into the dark. Spray tipped his face and the wind roared in his ears. He took a deep breath but it did no good. Someone threw a bottle from the deck above. It flashed past him and landed in the water. He saw the white of the splash but heard nothing above the throbbing of the ship. The damp came through to his elbows where he leaned on the rail and he shivered.

He had thought of not going home, of writing to his wife

to say that he was sick. But it seemed impossible for him not to do what he had always done. Besides she might have come to see him if he had been too sick to travel. Now he wanted to be at home among the sounds that he knew. Crows, hens clearing their throats and picking in the yard, the distant bleating of sheep on the hill, the rattle of a bucket handle, the slam of the back door. Above all he wanted to see the children. The baby, his favourite, sitting on her mother's knee, her tulle nightdress ripped at the back, happy and chatting at not having to compete with the others. Midnight and she the centre of attention. Her voice, hoarse and precious after wakening, talking as they turned the pages of the catalogue of toys they had sent for, using bigger words than she did during the day.

A man with a woollen cap came out onto the deck and leaned on the rail not far away. A sentence began to form in his mind, something to start a conversation. You couldn't talk about the dark. The cold, he could say how cold it was. He waited for the right moment but when he looked round the man was away, high stepping through the doorway.

He followed him in and went to the bar to get a drink before it closed. The girl was still there reading. The other girls were falling about and squawking with laughter at the slightest thing. They were telling in loud voices about former nights and about how much they could drink. Exaggerations. Ten vodkas, fifteen gin and tonic. He sat down opposite the girl reading and when she looked up from her book he smiled at her. She acknowledged the smile and looked quickly down at her book again. He could think of nothing important enough to say to interrupt her reading. Eventually when the bar closed she got up and left without looking at him. He watched the indentation in the cushioned moquette return slowly to normal.

He went back to his seat in the lounge. The place was smoke-filled and hot and smelt faintly of feet. The mongol was now asleep. With his eyes closed he became conscious of the heaving motion of the boat as it climbed the swell. She had said they were like tiny corkscrews. He thought of them boring into his wife's womb. He opened his eyes. A young woman's voice was calling incessantly. He looked to see. A toddler was running up and down the aisles playing.

'Ann-Marie, Ann-Marie, Ann-Marie! Come you back here!' Her voice rose annoyingly, sliding up to the end of the name. He couldn't see where the mother was sitting. Just a voice annoying him. He reached out his feet again to the vacant seat opposite and found he was still too short. To reach he would have to lie on his back. He crossed his legs and cradled his chin in the heart of his hand.

Although they were from opposite ends of the earth he was amazed that her own childhood in New Zealand should have sounded so like his own. The small farm, the greenness, the bleat of sheep, the rain. She had talked to him, seemed interested in him, how he felt, what he did, why he could not do something better. He was intelligent — sometimes. He had liked the praise but was hurt by its following jibe. She had a lot of friends who came to her flat — arty crafty ones, and when he stayed to listen to them he felt left outside. Sometimes in England his Irishness made him feel like a leper. They talked about books, about people he had never heard of and whose names he couldn't pronounce, about God and the Government.

One night at a party with ultra-violet lights someone with rings on his fingers had called him 'a noble savage'. He didn't know how to take it. His first impulse was to punch him, but up till that he had been so friendly and talkative — besides it was too Irish a thing to do. His nurse had come to his rescue and later in bed she had told him he must *think*. She had playfully struck his forehead with her knuckles at each syllable.

'Your values all belong to somebody else,' she had said.

He felt uncomfortable. He was sure he hadn't slept. He changed his position but then went back to cupping his chin. He must sleep.

'Ann-Marie, Ann-Marie.' She was loose again. By now they had turned the lights down in the lounge. The place was full of slumped bodies. The rows were back to back and some hitch-hikers had crawled onto the flat floor beneath the apex. He took his raincoat for a pillow and crawled into the free space behind his own row. Horizontal he might sleep. It was like a tent and he felt nicely cut off. In the next row some girls sat, not yet asleep. One was just at the level of his head and when she leaned forward to whisper her sweater rode up and bared a pale crescent of her lower back. Pale downy hairs moving into a seam at her backbone. He closed his eyes but the box containing the locket bit into his side. He turned and tried to sleep on his other side.

One night when neither of them could sleep his wife had said to him, 'Do you miss me when you're away?'

He said yes.

'What do you do?'

'Miss you.'

'I don't mean that. Do you do anything about it? Your missing me.'

'No.'

'If you ever do, don't tell me about it. I don't want to know.'

'I never have.'

He looked once or twice to see the girl's back but she was huddled up now sleeping. As he lay the floor increased in hardness. He lay for what seemed all night, his eyes gritty and tense, conscious of his discomfort each time he changed his position. The heat became intolerable. He sweated and felt it thick like blood on his brow. He wiped it dry with a handkerchief and looked at it to see. He was sure it must be morning. When he looked at his watch it said three o'clock. He listened to it to hear if it had stopped. The loud tick seemed to chuckle at him. His nurse had told him this was the time people died. Three o'clock in the morning. The dead hour. Life at its lowest ebb. He believed her. Walking the dimly lit wards she found the dead.

Suddenly he felt claustrophobic. The back of the seats closed over his head like a tomb. He eased himself out. His back ached and his bladder was bursting. As he walked he felt the boat rise and fall perceptibly. In the toilet he had to use the handrail. The smell of sick was still there.

How could his values belong to someone else? He knew what was right and what was wrong. He went out onto the deck again. The wind had changed or else the ship was moving at a different angle. The man who had rolled himself in his sleeping bag earlier in the night had disappeared. The wind and the spray lashed the seat where he had been sleeping. Tiny lights on the coast of Ireland winked on and off. He moved round to the leeward side for a smoke. The girl who had earlier been reading came out on deck. She mustn't have been able to sleep either. All he wanted was someone to sit and talk to for an hour. Her hair was untied now and she let it blow in the wind, shaking her head from side to side to get it away from her face. He sheltered his glowing cigarette in the heart of his hand. Talk·would shorten the night. For the first time in his life he felt his age, felt older than he was. He was conscious of the droop in his shoulders, his unshaven chin, his smoker's cough. Who would talk to him — even for an hour? She held her white raincoat tightly round herself, her hands in her pockets. The tail flapped furiously against her legs. She walked towards the prow, her head tilted back. As he followed her, in a sheltered alcove he saw the man in the sleeping bag, snoring, the drawstring of his hood knotted round his chin. The girl turned and came back. They drew level.

'That's a cold one,' he said.

'Indeed it is,' she said, not stopping. She was English. He had to continue to walk towards the prow and when he looked over his shoulder she was gone. He sat on an empty seat and began to shiver. He did not know how long he sat but it was better than the stifling heat of the lounge. Occasionally he walked up and down to keep the life in his feet. Much later going back in he passed an image of himself in a mirror, shivering and blue lipped, his hair wet and stringy.

In the lounge the heat was like a curtain. The sight reminded him of a graveyard. People were meant to be straight, not tilted and angled like this. He sat down determined to sleep. He heard the tremble of the boat, snoring, hushed voices. Ann-Marie must have gone to sleep — finally. That guy in the sleeping bag had it all worked out — right from the start. He had a night's sleep over him already. He tilted his watch in the dim light. The agony of the night must soon end. Dawn would come. His mouth felt dry and his stomach tight and empty. He had last eaten on the train. It was now six o'clock.

Once he had arranged to meet his nurse in the Gardens. It was early morning and she was coming off duty. She came to him starched and white, holding out her hands as she would to a child. Someone tapped him on the shoulder but he didn't want to look round. She sat beside him and began to stroke the inside of his thigh. He looked around to see if anyone was watching. There were two old ladies close by but they seemed not to notice. The park bell began to clang and the keepers blew their whistles. They must be closing early. He put his hand inside her starched apron to touch her breasts. He felt warm moistness, revolting to the touch. His hand was in her entrails. The bell clanged incessantly and became a voice over the Tannoy.

'Good morning, ladies and gentlemen. The time is seven o'clock. We dock at Belfast in approximately half an hour's time. Tea and sandwiches will be on sale until that time. We hope you have enjoyed your . . .'

He sat up and rubbed his face. The woman opposite, the mongol's mother, said good morning. Had he screamed out? He got up and bought himself a plastic cup of tea, tepid and weak, and some sandwiches, dog-eared from sitting overnight.

It was still dark outside but now the ship was full of the bustle of people refreshed by sleep, coming from the bathrooms with toilet bags and towels, whistling, slamming doors. He saw one man take a tin of polish from his case and begin to shine his shoes. He sat watching him, stale crusts in his hand. He went out to throw them to the gulls and watch the dawn come up.

He hadn't long to go now. His hour had come. It was funny the way time worked. If time stopped he would never reach home and yet he loathed the ticking, second by second slowness of the night. The sun would soon be up, the sky was bleaching at the horizon. What could he do? Jesus what could he do? If he could turn into spray and scatter himself on the sea he would never be found. Suddenly it occured to him that he *could* throw himself over the side. That would end it.

He watched the water sluicing past the dark hull forty feet below. 'The spirit is willing but the flesh is weak.' If only someone would take the whole thing away how happy he would be. For a moment his spirits jumped at the possibility of the whole thing disappearing — then it was back in his stomach heavier than ever. He put his face in his hands. Somehow it had all got to be hammered out. He wondered if books would solve it. Read books and maybe the problems won't seem the same. His nurse had no problems.

The dark was becoming grey light. They must have entered the Lough because he could see land now on both sides, like arms or legs. He lit a cigarette. The first of the day — more like the sixty-first of yesterday. He coughed deeply, held it a moment then spat towards Ireland but the wind turned it back in the direction of England. He smiled. His face felt unusual.

He felt an old man broken and tired and unshaven at the end of his days. If only he could close his eyes and sleep and forget. His life was over. Objects on the shore began to become distinct through the mist. Gasometers, chimney-stacks, railway trucks. They looked washed out, a putty grey against the pale lumps of the hills. Cars were moving and then he made out people hurrying to work. He closed his eyes and put his head down on his arms. Indistinctly at first, but with growing clarity, he heard the sound of an ambulance.

Umberto Verdi, Chimney Sweep

For Nan the smoking chimney had been the last straw. The cold wind had gusted all day and ten minutes after she had hung out a full wash, the line snapped. Nappies, vests, John's shirts, the lot were all lying on the muddy path in the garden. After she had gathered them up she promised herself a cup of coffee but even then, at her own fireside she didn't get peace. Every time one of the children closed the door or the wind roared outside, a billow of smoke curved down and out into the room. Now that she was there to watch the children she took away the fireguard. From where she sat, with her feet in the hearth, she could see the underside of the cream tiled mantlepiece blackened with soot. Tiny motes hung in the air — one hovered over her coffee and she shooed it away with her hand. Mary, the eldest of the four and the only one at school, came in and slammed the front door. A great cloud of acrid smoke belched round Nan, making her cough. She crashed the coffee cup down onto the mantlepiece, slopping it over, ran out into the hall and cuffed the child on the back of the head, shouting, 'How many times must I tell you not to slam doors?'

Mary snivelled away, dropping her school bag on the floor, to get herself a piece of bread and jam. Nan sat down on the bottom step next to the telephone and phoned the chimney sweep. When she was told she'd have to wait three weeks she said if he couldn't oblige her, in future she'd get somebody else to clean her chimney. Nan slammed the phone back into its cradle and pulled out the telephone directory, turning to yellow pages. As she ran her finger down the list of chimney sweeps she noticed the bad condition of her nails. They'd never been as bad as that before — even when she'd been in the wards. She must try to take more calcium, somehow. She found herself trying to choose the best name. They were all very ordinary, Greens, Parker, Smith, until she came to the last one: VERDI, Umberto. 'That's nice,' she thought and dialled the number. The tone buzzed for a long time. The baby crawled out to the foot of the stairs and began to cry. A woman's voice answered in an Italian accent and they arranged that Mr Verdi should come in two days' time at eleven o'clock.

'You must be his wife,' said Nan. Oh no, Umberto was not married. The baby clawed at her tights. 'Oh I see,' said Nan. 'Thank you,' and she rang off. She was now behind time and had to rush because John would be home soon, looking for his dinner. It was much later when she was washing the dishes that she found her half-finished coffee on the mantlepiece with its white disc of cold skin. She tipped it down the sink in disgust. If there was one thing she hated it was waste.

The next day she went shopping with the baby and Jane in the pram and Michael walking along, holding the handle. She thanked God that Mary had finally gone to school. All the groceries were stacked into the pram rack and Nan was about to go home when she hesitated outside the wine-store. She put the brake on the pram and took Michael and Jane by the hand into the shop. The crisp assistant smiled at her. 'How much is a bottle of Campari?' asked Nan. The assistant told her and she checked her purse. She could just afford it if she didn't pay the paper boy till next week. The bottle was wrapped up in brown paper with a neat twist at the top. Michael was kneeling, trying to peel the labels off some beer bottles on a bottom shelf and she dragged him out by the hand, scolding.

At home she pulled the paper off the bottle and looked at its colourful label and the clear scarlet liquid. She set the bottle on the top shelf well behind the sauces and pickles. She'd been for a holiday to the Italian Riveria long before she'd met John. The smells were what she had remembered most, romantic smells that were nearly bad smells, in the small back streets of the town. The peeling walls and shutters, the wrought iron balconies of the hotels in the old section draped with bathing suits and towels — and the boys, brown and beautiful, slapping along the streets in loose sandles and shorts, their shirts open down to the waist, smelling of sun-tan oil as they passed herself and the other girls sitting drinking Campari on the piazza of the hotel before lunch, laughing among themselves. The way they looked at you — nobody had looked at her like that, before or since. She gave a little shiver and a smile as she remembered.

She had to wash up what remained of the breakfast dishes before she could use the basin for peeling the potatoes. She could never get the sequence of things right. Day after day she would start the washing up and only then see that the bread had to be put away. The plastic lid of the bread bin would slip away from her wet fingers and clatter onto the floor and its crack would creep another inch towards the edge. She started peeling the potatoes. On the window sill in front of her stood a milk bottle full of tadpoles which John had collected for the children. She had watched the dots lengthen day by day, watched them change from stillness into life. She wondered if they lived on the jelly which surrounded them and what they did when they had eaten their way out of the egg. They were all wriggling and writhing now with their fully developed tails.

A screaming match had started up in the front room between Michael and Jane, and Nan had to rush in, her hands dripping wet. She settled it by giving them all a glass of lemonade even though it was too near dinner time.

Dr Kamel had been a great man for a glass of lemonade. She was surprised at herself remembering him now, as she stood over the sink. He had asked her out many times and even though he didn't mind her drinking, he was very strict with himself. His religion didn't allow alcohol, so he sat in the bars with her, his black face shining and sober, over a glass of lemonade. It was his manners that she liked. He always stood up when she came into the room, walked to the outside on the pavement, lit her cigarettes for her even though she sat at the far side of the room. He opened doors for her, held her hand coming down steps and a thousand other gestures that made her feel nice. John had been a bit like that before they were married but it was all gone now. He barged into rooms in front of her, had forgotten even to introduce her to new people, the few times they'd gone out together lately. At week-ends he refused to shave and would slop about in his oldest clothes and what she hated most was when he lay in bed, his hair tousled, almost till mid-day. Saturdays and Sundays he was more of a hindrance than a help because her whole routine was spoiled when she couldn't get the beds made in the morning. Whether there was anything wrong with it or not, week-ends he would work at the car and come in leaving oily marks in the sink and on the towels. Once she even had to clean the bar of soap after he'd washed his hands. With Kamel it would have been different.

The baby came crawling out to the kitchen and pulled at her leg to be lifted. She wiped his snuffly nose with the tail of her apron and carried him back into the front room, scolding the elder ones for letting him out. She stirred the murky water looking for the half-peeled potato. With Kamel it all might have been different.

The one and only time he had been to her home was the night he had proposed to her. Her mother had come in startled from the door and said that it must be somebody for her. Nan had gone in to the front room and Kamel was there, springing nervously to his feet. He had asked her to marry him, she had laughed, but then, when she saw how much this hurt him she became serious. He said that he was going back to the Sudan in a month's time and that he could wait a week for her answer. The gulf between their cultural backgrounds, he said, would be the main obstacle but that it would be an adventure for her to try and cross this gulf. To live in a new country, a place where it was sometimes so hot that it was necessary to soak one's clothes to keep cool — to sit and eat with her fingers out of the same bowl as the rest of his family. She could learn Arabic which he himself would delight to teach her. On Sundays it was necessary to wear the Jalabis, a long white garment similar to a night gown. Would not all this be an adventure? Although she already knew it, she said she would give him his answer by the end of the week. That night, as she lay tucked in behind John's back, Kamel's black face kept appearing, pleading, pointing to the deserts and the pyramids.

The next morning, after she had got John out to work and washed the breakfast dishes she phoned her neighbour two doors up and asked her if she could take the kids off her hands for an hour or so at eleven — only two of them. The baby would go for his sleep at that time. The soot and dust might affect Michael's A.S.T.H.M.A. She watched the boy's blank face remain blank as she spelt the word. Anyway they would be terribly in the way ... She would take them *all* morning. That was far *too* kind of her. Nan packed them off up the street and began tidying.

She went out to the shed to get some old newspapers. Just as she was covering the china cabinet she remembered that she might need some glasses. She carefully lifted out two champagne glasses with floral gold rims, a wedding present from Ward Ten, smelt that they were musty and took them to give them a wash. She lifted the Campari from behind the pickles and set it with the shining glasses.

At a quarter to eleven she put the baby up for his nap and, when up the stairs, decided she would change. She looked in the wardrobe and walked her fingers over the squeeze of dresses. There were things there she hadn't had on for ages. Dress frocks that she'd worn to formals — at a time when they went to formals — winter dresses, summer frocks. She picked a white dress, very plain except for the slightest silver border round the neckline. She could wear it, now that she was getting her figure back. Standing side on to the mirror she wondered if it was too short. In the bathroom she combed her hair, put on some make-up, not too much, just enough to give her a bit of colour, then went downstairs.

It was cool without the fire so she went into the back room and switched on the electric heater. Occasionally she came out to look through the front window, her arms folded. By now it was well after eleven and she wondered if he would come at all. The whole thing was keeping her back, she told herself. There was so much she could be going on with.

At half past eleven she went into the front room again and looked out the window. A chimney sweep had just propped his bicycle against the gatepost and was unstrapping the brushes that hung from the bar. A moment later he was knocking on the door. He was small and fat, fifty if he was a day, with trousers which came up to the middle of his chest. His face was black with soot and he raised his cap to her revealing a clean, pink, bald head. He knelt down in front of the fireplace untying his bundle of rods and spoke over his shoulder to Nan who had perched herself on the wooden arm of a chair.

'That's the quare day, missus,' he said. Nan nodded even though he couldn't see her. She was watching the rolls of fat creasing at the back of his neck as he tried to look up the chimney.

'Do you work for Umberto Verdi?' Nan asked.

'I am Umberto Verdi, I work for meself.' He smiled round at her.

'I didn't imagine you'd be . . . like . . . what you are.'

'What did you expect, missus?'

'I thought you'd be . . .' she hesitated. 'I thought you might have been a vacuum sweep.'

'None of these new fangled gadgets for me,' he said as he screwed the brush head to the first rod. 'You can't beat the brush.' He tried to push it up the chimney but it wouldn't go. He bent over and looked again.

'It's awkward,' said Nan. 'The last sweep says it is badly built.' Eventually he got the brush up and with quick flicks of his pudgy wrist attached new rods. A deep rumbling came from the chimney breast, as he shoved and pushed. Nan wondered if it would wake the baby upstairs, not that it mattered now.

After a time the sweep said, 'Would you like to go outside and see the brush sticking out the top?'

Nan laughed, 'I'm not a child, you know.'

'Just to prove the job is done, missus.'

'Oh,' said Nan, biting her lip and smiling. 'I'll believe you.'

He pulled the brush down again and swept the soot into the

large black cloth he had spread. She told him he could put it out at the bottom of the garden. When he came back into the kitchen she asked him if he wanted to wash his hands. 'The one bath at the end of the day does me,' he said. Seeing the tadpoles he leaned over the sink and looked closely at the bottle.

'I saw a programme about those. They said you shouldn't take them out of the ponds.' He clinked the bottle with his horny fingernail and the tadpoles panicked and wriggled in all directions at once. Nan stood, her purse in her hand and when he told her the price she gave him two shillings extra. She thought him a nice man with a nice smile. He lifted his cap showing his pink dome again and moved into the room to gather up his rods.

After he had gone she cleared the papers, noticing that there wasn't a pick of soot or dirt anywhere. After the crackling of the papers the quiet of the house unnerved her a bit but it was pleasant for a change. She opened the Campari, poured herself a glass and sagged down into a seat in the front room. She held its crimson up to the light. It was sweet and when swallowed had an acrid after taste which she had forgotten about. She couldn't remember which one of the girls it was who said that she had tasted nicer medicines. Whoever it was, she had no taste. After two more sips she wondered if maybe she hadn't got a bad bottle, or if perhaps it was supposed to be taken with white lemonade. She went out to the kitchen and tipped the little that was left in the glass down the sink. Maybe John would take the rest of it.

When she was changing back into her other clothes she must have wakened the baby. When she went in, the room was filled with a soiled nappy smell. Downstairs the phone rang. She tucked the baby under her arm and raced to answer it. It was the neighbour from two doors up. Michael had fallen and bumped his head and couldn't be consoled, so much so that she was afraid that he might have an A.T.T.A.C.K. Would it be all right to send them both back as she had noticed that the chimney sweep had left. Nan said yes and left the front door open so that she wouldn't have to get up again to let them in when they came.

Where the Tides Meet

We arrive at Torr Head about an hour before dusk and get out
of the car. Three men, Christopher the boy, and the dog.
Michael and Martin stand, their guns broken, loading them with
bright, brick-red cartridges from their pockets. We have lost
the dog's lead and I use a makeshift choker. It is an ordinary
lead but I form a noose with the loop of the handle so that
when he pulls too hard the noose tightens.

'For God's sake don't let him go,' they tell me. He is too
eager and pulls me at a run when I want to walk. They tell me
to tap him on the nose and shout 'heel' and he will respond.
He is too eager. They keep their guns broken and climb the
fence. The boy Christopher is excited and anxious and edges
ahead to try and see. He is on tip-toe trying to see over the
next rise. Michael, his father hisses at him, 'Keep behind the
line of the guns.' I walk behind all three with the dog. It is a
black labrador called Ikabod. His tongue hangs out as he
strains forward. I must be leaning at an angle of forty-five de-
grees trying to hold him. The makeshift lead is so embedded into the black folds of his neck that the only part of it visible is
the taut line to my hand. The chain at my end bites deeply.

Suddenly Martin shouts, not a loud shout, but a quiet
urgent one, 'Mickey, to your right.'

Michael brings the gun up to his cheek, leans slightly forward, all balance. The sound is half way between a crack and a
thud. The barrel jerks slightly as he fires. Both barrels. It is
only then that I see the white scuts of two rabbits disappearing into some bushes on our right. At the sound of the gun

Ikabod goes mad. He pulls me running and sliding down the hill. On the point of falling I decide to let him go. If Michael has hit one of the rabbits it must be the dog's job to retrieve. Ikabod disappears into the bushes, the lead whipping after him loosely. It is only then that I hear Michael shouting, 'Hold on to him.' I hear two more shots and my head ducks down into my coat, thinking Martin is shooting over my head at the same two rabbits, but when I look round he is shooting up the hill. I don't see what he is shooting at. I go down and look over the bush. It is a sloping cliff of rocks covered in bushes and grasses. Ikabod runs hither and thither looking for the rabbits. I whistle at him and he comes back. He is a good dog. Christopher is beside me looking over, 'Did he get one? Did he get one?' We catch up with the others.

I say defending myself, 'If you don't let him off after you shoot when *do* you let him off?'

'You don't,' says Michael.

'What did we bring him for then?' He doesn't answer. 'I thought he was supposed to be a retriever.'

'For birds,' says Michael and everybody laughs. Both men are pushing cartridges into their guns. We stand a while and talk, scanning the hillside yet knowing we have scared everything within earshot.

'You don't expect to see something that soon,' says Martin. Michael, who has been here many times before, points out the sea where the tides meet. Just beyond Torr Head the sea is white and swirling. Waves leap and crash together as if onto rocks but there are no rocks. This is about two hundred yards off-shore. They tell me it is the Irish sea coming up and the Gulf Stream coming down. In a boat they say you would have no chance.

We double back to a field on the actual Torr itself where they have seen rabbits before. Each fence they break their guns. Each fence Ikabod tries to go through the wire and me over it so that there is an elaborate disentangling and tugging each time. We have reached the field now and they walk in front of me, spread out, Christopher nearer to his father than Martin. The grass is coarse and long but flattened by the wind which must be constant in this place. It has the appearance of grass by a river in flood. The men walk with their guns at the ready, chest high. They stride, but stride quietly, their head turning from side to side sweeping the landscape. I think to myself that they are like hunters and only then realise that that is what they are. We reach the Torr itself without seeing anything or a shot being fired. We stop and talk. Michael asks me if I would like a shot. I say yes, I let the dog off the lead, he runs mad.

'What is there to shoot at?' He points out an old fence post, a railway sleeper, at the edge of the cliff. He shows me the safety catch. I click it off and take aim. It has begun to get dark and the sea behind the post is slate grey. Flints of white from where the tides meet distract me. The butt seems remarkably close to my cheek and I know to expect the recoil of the gun. I am afraid of it and when I shoot I miss completely. We inspect the post. The noise of the explosion pinging still in my ears.

'I did hit it,' I say.

Michael looks closer. 'It's fucking woodworm.' He keeps his voice low so that the boy will not hear. The few small holes do look like woodworm. I go back and shoot the other barrel. I miss again. Martin has gone off looking for more rabbits. We hear a shot from over the brow of the hill. It sounds distorted, plucked away by the wind. Michael loads the gun and fires at the post. It gouges a small crater in the dead wood. Around the periphery when I look closely there are some holes like woodworm.

'Mine's a pint.'

It must be two fields before we notice that Ikabod isn't with us. We stand whistling and shouting but he does not come. We go back to the fence post and look all round, calling.

'Would he have gone over the cliff?' We climb the small fence edging very carefully down the slippy grass.

'Ik-a-bod, Ik-a-bod.' Then we hear a definite dog noise from below.

'He's there somewhere.' We do not know whether it is a cliff like the last one with bushes and outcrops and paths so we inch forward with care. I get to the edge first. It is a sheer drop. Emptiness for about two hundred feet. A rook sails past on a level with us. There is a rubble of rocks below on the beach. I see Ikabod lying on his side at the bottom. From then on we do not talk. To our right there is an accessible way down to the beach and we run. By now the boy and Martin have caught up with us. We half slide, half run down the slope holding onto the tussocky grass. When we get to the dog it is dead. I put my hand on its side and find it still warm. There is no heartbeat. Christopher talks incessantly asking, 'Is it dead, Daddy. Is it dead?' He brushes against a tall weed and seeds fall from it onto the dog's fur. I take my hand away quickly, irrationally thinking of fleas leaving their dead host. Michael stands looking down at the dead dog. I look up to tell him that it is dead and see that he is crying. The wind is cuffing his hair, blowing it about his face. He cannot answer Christopher's questions.

He hunkers down beside the dog and I hear him saying, 'Fuck it,' again and again. There is no blood, just a string of saliva which has touched on some rocks. He reaches over and undoes the dog's collar, then begins to put rocks on top of the dog. In silence everybody helps. The skin seems mobile when heavy stones are placed on it. Eventually the dog is covered with a cairn and we stand back feeling a ridiculous need for prayer. Christopher does not cry out but keeps watching his father, doing everything that he does except cry. As we turn away Michael says, 'You get very attached to a hound,' almost by way of apology for his crying.

On the way back to the car in darkness, we string out, a single file, about ten yards between each of us, coming together only to help one another over fences.

Hugo

'I'm sure you're walking on air,' my mother said to Paul at his wedding. He was indeed in a joyful mood and he seemed to communicate it to all those around him.' But isn't it sad Hugo couldn't be here.'

Paul shrugged. The remark produced a sobering effect on him.

'Mother,' I said. 'This is neither the time nor the place.' The curtness of my remark, combined with an empty sherry glass, sent my mother away. Together Paul and I began to talk of old times and this led inevitably to Hugo's tragic end. Between us we fruitlessly tried to arrive at some sort of explanation. Paul seemed to see it only in terms of a simple sadness, nodding his head partly in sympathy, partly in disbelief, whereas I knew it to be a tragedy of a different order. Eventually Paul had to rise and excuse himself and go and look after his other guests.

Hugo's life and mine had intersected briefly and this had had an effect on me out of all proportion to its duration.

My father died when I was eight and it was only at about the age of fourteen that I felt the need of him. I wanted someone I could talk to, someone who would, with wisdom, answer the questions which racked me at this particular time. Someone who would give me confidence to overcome my stammering, someone whom I could ask about the complexities of love and the horrors of sex, someone who could tell me how to dress properly, someone who knew what it was right to like in Art.

My father had an old gramophone on which he played

Schubert piano with pine needles. Huge shellac records, with a red circle and a white dog singing into a horn, which whirred with static but which induced a calm in me, as a child, which I have not known since. When they were finished, after about two minutes, the tick of the over-run seemed the vilest sound in the world. The clack of teeth after divine music.

Ever since I could remember there had hung on the parlour wall two framed pen and wash drawings of people unknown to me, signed by my father. I thought them good but they lacked something. Alone I would stare at them for hours and try to find words for their shortcomings. Between these two drawings was a tiny picture, sent from the missions, of an oriental Madonna whose robe was made of butterfly wings — deep changing torquoise. I used to think how perfect the natural colour was, surrounded as it was by the gauche, cut-out form of the madonna. Nature achieves what is right without knowing.

We lived in a large old terrace house with four bedrooms in an area of the city which had seen better days, judging by the handles in the bedrooms for calling the maids. I was an only child and used a bedroom and a playroom, which was later to become the study. Shortly after my father died Mother decided, not being qualified to do anything else, to take in boarders to try and supplement her widow's pension.

We then had a succession of faceless men, bank clerks in blue suits, an insurance man who was granted the special privilege of leaving his bike in the hallway, a bald teacher whom mother asked to leave one day after some difficulty she had in making his bed. The bathroom shelf held an array of shaving brushes and razors and the house smelt of sweat and cigarette smoke.

Then Paul arrived, a pharmacy student, and became a favourite of my mother's. He had charm and the good looks and height of a Gregory Peck. He would bring her small presents from the country after he had been home for a week-end, a dozen new laid eggs wrapped in twists of newspaper with the hen's dirt still on them or a few pots of home-made gooseberry jam, labelled and dated. My mother really appreciated these gestures.

'A bank clerk,' she said, 'would never think of it in a thousand years.' He had a mouth-organ which he played with some skill, although I did not agree with his choice of music, popular melodies and country and western tunes.

After about a year of Paul's stay one of our bank-clerks decided to get married to a girl with thick legs whom I had pushed past many nights, *in flagrante*, at the doorway. Paul asked my mother if, as a special favour, she would take in one of his friends who was at that time living in dreadful digs with a harridan of a landlady. Mother flinched a little at the words 'digs' and 'landlady' but she could refuse Paul nothing.

'If he's anything like you Paul, he'll do,' she said. Paul laughed and said he wasn't a bit like him because he would cause her no trouble.

This was Hugo. I first saw him in the kitchen on the day he arrived. He was small, much smaller than Paul, slope shouldered, wearing a good Sunday suit, sitting with his knees together. His eyes darted behind his thick-lensed glasses at me as I came through the door. His face was narrow, twig-like, his nose like tweeked out plasticine and a thin neck with a large Adam's apple which jerked when he swallowed. 'Fatten him up,' were Paul's orders to my mother. Afterwards, when I became interested in such things, I found that he bore a facial resemblance to Joyce.

'Have you met Hugo?' my mother said. 'He's come to stay with us for a while.' I set my schoolbag in the corner and hung up my blazer.

'Hugo is a pharmacy student too,' Mother said. 'Paul told him what a good house this was to stay in. Wasn't that nice of him?' I nodded.

'Any homework?' she asked. 'Well, get it done then — before you start any nonsense.'

I cut myself a slab of bread, spread it with jam and bit a half moon out of it. I started my Maths. Hugo sat, still in the same position. He looked as if he was waiting for his tea.

'What is it?' he asked from the corner. I held up the book to show him. He came over to the table and looked at the problem. I have always found integration difficult. He sat in the chair beside me and guided me through the exercise in half the time I would normally have taken. Crumbs gathered in the spine of the exercise book and I blew them away before closing it. He proceeded to help me with my Latin, French and Physics homework, always explaining and illuminating.

He turned out to be quiet and thoughtful with a great sense of the ridiculous. He spoke in a thick regional accent, almost always self-deprecatingly. When he laughed it wasn't a guffaw like Paul's, the head thrown back. Actually his head bent forward onto his chest and he shook quietly as if suppressing a laugh. I have consulted Roget on this point and cannot find a suitable word to describe Hugo's laugh. Words for quiet laughter carry with them associations of sleaziness — 'snigger', 'snicker'. Roget also gives 'giggle' and 'titter' but these are frivolous. 'Chuckle' is the nearest but it is so inaccurate as to be almost useless. So I must content myself with 'laugh'.

It was shortly after he arrived that I saw it demonstrated. Paul was beginning to worry about being flabby and out of condition and had invested in a book on Yoga. My mother had looked at the pictures in the book and had kidded him that he wouldn't be able to do a single one. After tea Paul, Hugo and I went into the parlour to see if we could do some of the poses. I was able for some of them, probably because of my age and suppleness, but Paul rolled about the carpet grunting and gasping and twisting himself. Finally with some help from Hugo, who pushed his legs into position, he managed to complete 'the plough'. He was lying on his back with his legs, at the ankle, touching behind his head. The seat of his trousers was taut and shining. Paul, in a strangled voice, gasped to me to go and get my mother. She came, drying her hands on her apron, to see the feat. By this time Paul's face was almost purple, clamped as it was between his ankles.

'Bet you can't hold it for another thirty seconds,' my mother said.

'I can,' gasped Paul. Everyone waited, watching him. Then suddenly and quite distinctly he farted, a small piping accidental note. Laughing deafeningly his body sprung back and he lay exhausted and convulsed on the floor. Mother was screeching mock horror and abuse at him. Hugo fell into the armchair, his chin on his chest, and shook helplessly. When we had all recovered, my mother wiping her eyes with the tail of her apron and Paul shaking his head in disbelief that it should have happened to him, we noticed Hugo still laughing silently and uncontrollably in his armchair. This started us all off again. Even at supper-time Hugo was seen to be still laughing uproariously into himself.

About two months after this someone called at the door for Paul and I ran upstairs to the bedroom to see if he was in. He wasn't but Hugo was sitting in the middle of the floor in his underpants in the position of complete repose, index fingers and thumbs joined, hands relaxed and upturned, legs crossed. His head was bent down and he seemed to be barely breathing. I tend to move quietly about the house and he did not notice me. I said nothing to him and went back down the stairs to the door.

I have looked long and hard at this early period to try and read something into it of the tragedy that was to follow, but can find nothing. No prefiguring whatsoever. The only thing, looking back on it with hindsight, I took to be an indication of his state of mind — and even this is scientifically suspect — was the nature of his sleep.

Our last remaining bank clerk, Harry Carey, would occasionally decide to go home for the week-end. That would leave a bed free in the room with Paul and Hugo and I used to plague my mother to let me sleep with the boys. At first she steadfastly refused, then one day Paul overheard me asking, when Harry had gone home, and he persuaded her.

'Sure. Let him sleep in our room if he enjoys the crack.' he said.

'Well then, if *you* don't mind. It's just for one night now. It's not to be a regular occurrence.'

But it was. Every time that Harry went home I moved in with Paul and Hugo and would lie awake until they would come to bed — even if they were out at a dance — and listen to their talk far into the small hours of the morning. Paul would sit up wearing no pyjama jacket and smoke in bed. In the dark each time he drew on his cigarette his chin and nose would be lit by a red glow. The room smelt great and grown up.

'That blonde had her eye on you, Qugo,' said Paul.

'Which one?' said Hugo. Apart from the implied self-aggrandisment in the remark it seemed there had been a shapely blonde whom Hugo had tapped on the shoulder and asked to dance. When she turned round she had a terrible squint.

I heard the crackle of sweet papers mixed with Hugo's wheezing laugh. He asked me if I'd like one. Paul struck a match and by its light I caught the sweet thrown to me. Between crunchings Hugo tried to answer the question Paul had just put to him. What would he look for in his ideal woman? Often I fell asleep to the sound of his voice.

One of the nights I slept with them I was awakened for some reason and could not get back to sleep again. Suddenly I heard a noise which terrified me. A mixture of grating and squeaking, a wild sound, not loud, which created a nausea in me as a sharp tin edge scraping along marble or brick. The room went quiet again. I thought the sound came from the direction of Hugo's bed. It came again, this time louder. I crept from bed trying to trace the sound. In the dark it came again and again. I switched on the bedside light and looked at Hugo's face. A knot of muscle gathered at the elbow of his jaw and vibrated, then his whole lower jaw moved slowly from side to side and the noise came. Hugo was grinding his teeth as he slept. Flints in a slow rub of terrible pressure. It was a sound quite unlike anything I have heard before or since. He looked pale and unrecognizable without his glasses, his hair tousled. It was only after what seemed like hours that he stopped this gnashing and I was able to sleep.

He told me later that he had very bad teeth, half rotten he said, but seemed pleased that Joyce had suffered from the same complaint.

It was at about this time that Hugo began to help me to conquer my stammer. My mother had sent me to elocution and speech therapy but it had done little good. I still got stuck. I hated the woman who taught me, with her red mouth pulsing like a sea anenome.

'Watch my lips. Now say oo... oo... oo.' She wore thick scarlet lipstick. I did not want to do things well for her so I failed.

I was hoovering the stairs one day and singing at the same time. Even though I got pocket money for it, it was a task that I enjoyed. The hoover created a two tone base note, one when idling, the other a fraction higher when the sucking end was pressed into the carpet. Around this base I would sing songs. One that was accompanied pretty well was 'I know that my Redeemer liveth' from the *Messiah* and I was singing it at the top of my voice, which incidentally was just beginning to break, when Hugo came up behind me. He mimed applause over the noise of the hoover when I had finished.

When the cleaning was over he asked me what was the first line of the aria I was singing.

'N... N... N... I know thu... thu... that my Redeemer l... le... le.'

'Y'see,' he interrupted me. 'You can sing it perfectly but you can't say it.'

I was embarrassed. No one had ever said this to me before. Only my mother and my speech therapist ever spoke openly about it. Everyone else waited or, what was worse, helped me out: I got up to try and leave the room.

'Wait a minute,' Hugo called after me. 'C'mere.' I stopped. 'If you're going to be a man of ideas you must be able to articulate in some way. At the moment, with the stammering, you're only giving yourself half a chance. I know its not your problem but you know these people who tell you that they're full up to here of *something*, ideas, emotions, feelings. Ask them to put a name on it and they just shrug and look intense. You must be able to speak it or write it — and if you can't it's not a thought. It's an urge — like dogs have. Look at Paul,' he said and went into kinks of laughter, 'he can speak from both ends. So, lad, we must get you speaking.'

He treated my problem simply and openly and told me he had devised a therapy which might help me. He claimed that he was trying to cure me by the 'rhythm method', which he seemed to think funny. Firstly he got me to sing the line. Then he would get me to establish a slow rhythm by tapping my finger on the table and breaking the words up into syllables which corresponded to the beat. Gradually I would speed the rhythm and the word would come with it. Later in these lessons, in which I showed considerable improvement, I dispensed with beating on the table and would secretly tap my foot as if to music. As the months went by my performance became more and more presto. Then all outward signs of rhythm disappeared and by the following Christmas I could talk for long periods without stoppage — two or three sentences at a time, even though they sounded monotonous and had little cadence. Even today when I am nervous before giving a lecture to my students I take several deep breaths and behind the secrecy of the tilted lectern establish a tapping rhythm with my finger, then I start.

Let me pause for a moment, now that I have my story launched, to try and explain both what I am trying to do and why I am doing it. For a start, it is not a story. What has happened cannot in the truest sense be said to be fiction, but the telling of a life, which is biography. At this point I must admit to having had great difficulty writing the foregoing pages. I have never experienced this before in writing but then I have never tried to write anything like this. When I sit down to write a critical article or a lecture the words seem to flow from my pen. Indeed my first job is to limit them. To enshrine my ideas in as few words as possible is my aim. Here I am doing the opposite, trying to swell a few fragments into something substantial. I am not entirely new in this field of course. My publication on Sir Aubrey de Vere (1788-1846) is biography of a sort, but there the family gave me access to all the papers, letters, diaries and unpublished poems. Now I have nothing but some memories to work on.

One of the most difficult adjustments I have had to make is with regard to the way I write. I find it awkward to attenuate my normal style. For me to write simply is unnatural and as arduous as thinning a forest.

Why should I write it at all? Perhaps to show something of

my respect, perhaps to assuage my guilt. I owe it to Hugo. If it had not been for the novel he had written I don't believe I would be trying to articulate what I think.

I know what a doubtful quality sincerity is when I find it in a piece of literature. The critic in me screams, 'It is unimportant' — now a voice in me says equally loudly, 'If I am not sincere what I am doing is worthless.' Similarly in literature adherence to the truth, the facts as they actually happened, is of no value and yet I intend to be as close to truth as my memory will permit. I must be honest.

One day when Paul and Hugo were studying for their final exams they decided to take the afternoon off and go for a walk. When I asked them they agreed to take me along, telling my mother it was no bother. We walked over the Cave Hill which dominates the town, a forested place, and the two men talked. Then after a while Paul turned to me and said, 'And what are you going to do with your life? They say you're a boy genius.'

'I d... d... don't know,' I said. 'I think I want to go to you... you... university.'

'Ah, but what will you do? Which particular branch do you intend to honour with your presence?' I was a bit embarrassed by the way he spoke to me but I answered him nonetheless.

'I think I want to do something in.. in.. the Humanities. I'm curious. . .'

'You're mad. Science is the only thing with any future. Like it or not, boy, in the world you've got to earn your living.' said Paul. 'And the best way to do it is with a BSc under your belt. If you have curiosity how could you be anything *but* a scientist?'

'I will wait and see what subjects I do well in. I'm doing 'A' le... le... le...'

'Levels,' said Paul.

A bird sang in the wood 'ch... ch... ch...' mocking me.

'In English, L... L... Latin, Physics and Chemistry — so I can still shoose.'

'Who's that fella to say. Don't heed him,' said Hugo. 'Science looks at the surface of things. If you have any real curiosity read Philosophy or Literature. Paul, there, has a headful of cells — mine is slightly different,' and here he laughed. 'Besides, the academic world of Science can be very vicious and narrow-minded. They'd cut your throat to publish a paper. I've seen them at work.'

'Where would the world be today without its scientists?' cried Paul.

'You're not often right, Paul,' said Hugo, 'but you're wrong this time. Look at those trees.' The sun tilted into the depths of the forest to our right, flecking the ground with yellow and brown. The remains of bluebells covered the forest floor with a film of petrol blue. 'Just look. A scientist can tell us about phloem and xylem and tap roots and chromosomes but he can't tell us what it looks like or feels like. This is rubbish anyway. There is no argument between the Arts and Sciences. That's over long ago. What we're talking about is the lad here. What is best for him. Which subject are you happiest at?'

'I thought you were a pharmacist,' I said to Hugo.

'So I am.'

'Then why do you talk as if you knew all about the Humanities?'

Paul answered for him. 'Hugo has a lot of skeletons hanging in his cupboard.' Here he cupped his hand over his mouth and hissed, 'Qugo reads books.' When Paul wanted to tease him he pronounced his name with a Q. Hugo responded by ignoring him.

'Literature is the science of feeling. The artist analyses what feelings are, then in some way or other he tries to reproduce in the reader those same feelings. How much more subtle an experiment than overflowing an oul' bath. How many feelings are there to reproduce, d'ye think? Is there a periodic classification of feelings? Nuances. That's the secret. The lines in the spectrum between pity and sympathy. Literature is the space between words. It fills the gaps that language leaves. English has only one word for love and yet how many different types of love are there in Literature?'

Paul laughed and put his arm around Hugo's shoulders as if offering him to me.

'This is Hugo at his best,' he said. 'Take him or leave him. There's not another idiot like him.'

When Hugo had been talking his face had been serious and intense. He kept adjusting his glasses on the bridge of his nose. Now when Paul presented him he laughed and the conversation turned away from my future to something else.

In all the time I knew him Hugo never collected books. He had no bookshelf — no, that is wrong — he had a bookshelf but it contained only his pharmacy textbooks, great thick volumes honeycombed with benzene rings with their pendant NH_2's and their off shoots of OH's and HPO_4's. Afterwards I discovered that the public library was the source for his vast reading. It was rare to mention a book he had not read. Sometimes, when I was tracking down something for an essay not available in our own university library I would see him ensconced in a corner of the reference section, reading. I made it a point of always going over and having a few words with him.

It was shortly after the conversation in the woods that we discovered that Paul had failed his finals. Hugo had passed with high commendation. There was a palpable atmosphere of depression pervading the house. It was the first time that I had ever seen Paul gloomy. He sat in the chair, his handsome face unshaven, smoking and staring out the kitchen window at the tip of the backyard wall. Hugo had to control his elation at doing so well, but he was genuinely sorry for Paul. I had just finished my 'A' levels and felt confident of doing well.

'Next year for sure,' Hugo said to Paul.

'That's what gets me — doing that boring stuff all over again.'

'Yeah, I know,' said Hugo.

'Failing stinks,' said Paul. 'When I saw that board my guts just fell on the ground. It's almost as if it's personal. They're saying you're not good enough. Christ and I worked so *hard*.'

'I know — but there's worse things you could fail at,' said Hugo.

'I don't know what they are.' Paul paused to bite his nails. 'But it's great about you. I'm really pleased for you. What are you going to do?'

'Taggart says he'll keep me on, so I have a job. I think I'll stay on here as well and give you a hand next year.'

I ran out excited to tell Mother that Hugo and Paul would be staying on a further year.

On reading over what I have written so far I feel I have created a false picture of Hugo. Because I wanted to record, as exactly as I could remember, what he said I give the impression that he was talkative and gregarious. This was not so. For long periods — weeks on end — I would never hear him say a word, apart from what was required by good manners. He would seem morose, eating his meals and disappearing into the bedroom or going out for long walks on his own. At times like these I noticed that Paul left him alone, would talk if required but would not initiate any conversation to resurrect Hugo from his mood. During the year after he passed his finals this isolation happened with increasing frequency. Paul told me, many years afterwards, that this was when he was working flat out on the novel. My mother even began to remark his taciturnity.

'That lad hasn't a word to throw to a dog, this weather. I'll be glad to see the back of him when he goes.'

She hadn't long to wait because the following spring Hugo announced that he was moving out. Now that he was earning he had managed to get himself a mortgage and he had bought a house, not too far from where we lived. He said that he was bringing his family there to live. I was surprised at him having a family because he had never really mentioned them. It was something with which I hadn't really associated him. When he left he bought Mother a pearl necklace and she took back all that she had said about him.

'A queer fish but a good hearted lad.'

By this time I was in my first year at University, studying English Literature and before he left we had some good talks about Joyce. *The Portrait of the Artist* was one of the books I was studying. It transpired that he knew a tremendous amount about Joyce, had read every word that he had written and almost every word that had been written about him. At the time one problem that seemed to occupy him more than any other was Joyce's daughter who was now in a mad house somewhere in England. He claimed Joyce had made a sacrificial victim of her for the cause of Art. He had dragged her around the Continent from Paris to Trieste to Zurich, giving her no security, no home, no life until eventually she went mad. Joyce blamed himself for her state for ever afterwards.

'But then, d'ye think,' said Hugo, 'would it have been better if Joyce had settled in Rathgar and never written a word? His wee girl might have been normal. Would the world be a richer or a poorer place? Would you rather have Joyce with a normal daughter or *Ulysses?*'

'I know what answer you would get,' I said, 'if you asked Joyce's daughter that question.'

'A good point,' he laughed, then became serious. 'There is no doubt in my mind which I would choose.'

He helped me considerably with *The Portrait*, giving me insights into the book which, I think, my tutors and lecturers would have been incapable of.

'May I come and see you sometime in your house?' I asked.

'We could meet in a pub some night, if you like. D'ye drink yet?'

'Sure,' I said, although two pints was about my limit. 'But don't tell my mother.'

I didn't see him again until the night of Paul's celebration on passing his finals but did not get talking seriously to him because the room was crowded and noisy and everybody was tipsy.

Some months later I had volunteered to do a seminar on 'A Painful Case', one of Joyce's stories from *Dubliners* and I thought I would get Hugo's views on the subject. I got his address, which he had left with my mother for forwarding his mail, and went round one evening after tea.

It was a smallish house in a terrace. Paper blinds were pulled on all the windows like a dead house. I rang the bell and an oldish woman answered. Her grey hair stood out from her head like she'd had an electric shock. She smiled broadly.

'Is Hugo there?' I asked. She closed the door over, leaving me standing on the step, and went away. Hugo came to the door nervously pulling at the waist of his Fairisle jumper.

'Come in, come in,' he said. He seemed confused and embarrassed. He stopped in the hallway and leaned against the wall. 'What can I do for you?'

'I just thought we could have that drink. Something else about Joyce has come up. I'd like your opinion on it.'

'I'll have to shave,' he said rubbing his chin. 'Come in and wait.' Then he turned conspiratorially and whispered, 'In here.'

At that moment the woman with the electric hair opened the door of the other room and said, 'Who's your little friend, Hugo? Am I not going to meet him?'

Hugo introduced me to his mother and going out said he would be as quick as he could. It was the end of a summer day and a chill was in the air. Hugo's mother was kneeling trying to light the fire. On the side-board and pinned to the wall I could just see in the gloom unframed paintings. Childish abstracts and several crude attempts to paint what I took to be Don Quixote and Sancho Panza.

'So your mother looked after my Hugo for three years?' she said.

'That's r... r... r... right.'

'Very well she did it too. He was never happier. He's losing weight now. I can't look after him.' She said all these quick sentences over her shoulder.

'Are you any good at fires? No, I suppose not.' The fire had gone out at the first attempt. Now she was spoonfulling sugar from a bowl over the top of the coals. She bundled papers and put them on top of the coal and lit them.

'I think it is easier to light if the coal is warm,' she said. The flames from the papers roared up the chimney and went out. The sugar melted and bubbled a bit, then went brown. Quixote's white horse was stick-like and flat. Sancho's mule was even more badly drawn, if that was possible, and its colour had gone all muddy.

'Firelighters are great,' said the old woman. 'But we haven't got any. I think they stink the house.'

Suddenly the door opened and with relief I looked round expecting to see Hugo, but it was someone else — a boy of about my own age, wearing the exact same Fairisle jumper as Hugo had on two minutes ago. The boy looked subnormal, blunted features, eyes vacant and twitching. He spoke in a thick, unrecognizable speech. 'Oo da.'

The mother introduced me to Hugo's brother and I shook hands with him. He laughed, spittle shining on his chin, and seemed delighted to see me. Hugo seemed to take hours shaving. I was damp with sweat and the minute he came into the room I stood up, ready to go. Hugo's brother reached out his arms and said something which I couldn't begin to interpret. Hugo went over to him and ruffled his hair and hugged him kindly with one arm.

'Sure, Bobby, sure,' he said. When we left, the fire was still unlit. Outside the evening was fresh and clear.

'What did your brother want?' I asked.

'I'd promised him we'd paint.'

'Did he do the Quixotes on the wall?'

'No, they're mine,' said Hugo. I felt very embarrassed but he did not seem to mind at all that I should have ascribed his paintings to his subnormal brother.

'You're a primitive,' I said, trying to get out of the situation gracefully.

'If you say so. Bobby likes to paint. It's a kind of therapy for him as well. When I paint I encourage him to paint with me. He's improving.'

'Yes.'

'You'll have to forgive my mother. She's a bit odd. She's had a lot to put up with in her life, what with Bobby and things.'

One of the things, I later found out from Paul, was that Hugo's father had committed suicide by putting his head in the gas oven.

In the pub we sat down to pints.

'How's the job?' I asked.

'Which one?'

Taggart had given him the sack. He had got a job in another

shop but had left it. Now he was just doing locums.

'There's more money in it,' he said. 'I've realized I just hate the public. They come into the shop snivelling and coughing with their eyes on the ground. Nothing is important for them. They're so stupid. I hate when you make a joke — you know, intentionally — and you are serving a fool who thinks you haven't been aware of what you've said. Then he tries to underline it with some remark and claims the joke for his own. Do you know what I mean?' It's like a fully grown man being proud of finding the six sweeties hidden in the picture. I can't think of an example off-hand yet it happens a hundred times a day. They have no intelligence themselves so they don't expect to find it in others.'

'A job's a job,' I said.

'I can't be smooth and charming like Paul. People think I am dour. Taggart just thought I was insolent, the bastard. I've applied for a job in a hospital pharmacy. You don't have to meet people there.'

As we drank he became more and more talkative. He told me things about himself which I never knew. He had gone away for a time to study for the priesthood. He had been a journalist for a year on a small provincial paper. Then he confessed to having written a novel. I was very excited by this news.

'You must let me read it.'

'I might someday. It's about 250,000 words but I'm not sure if it's finished yet.'

'Wow, that's some size. What is it about?'

'I don't like to talk about it. But if I do let you read it you'll have to be honest.' I nodded that I would be. 'I don't want just to be good. I want my book to be *great*. It has to be.' He laughed and said, 'That's the drink talking now.'

'Will you not tell me what it is about?' I asked again.

'No. But I might give you a clue.'

I bought a drink for him but none for myself. I was becoming groggy and wanted to listen to what he had to say.

'It's all a matter of juxtapositions. Intersections might be a better word. Two things happen together and we get more than double the result.'

'Like Joyce's Epiphanies?'

'Yes, a bit like that, but not the same. One recent one was — I was in the grounds of a monastery at this open air mass and there was a pop group playing the hymns very badly and just in front of me was a rose bush. It hadn't flowered but the buds were green and covered with greenfly. The leaves were riddled with holes and there were rust spots all over them. That's the kind of thing I mean. Both flawed but something different arising out of the joining of the experiences.'

'I think I see,' I said.

'You don't sound convinced.' He laughed into his beer.' The one unforgettable one — and this one is in the novel — happened to me on a train once in England. I was in a seat opposite what looked like two soldiers, short haircuts sandpapered up the back, tatoos on their arms. It was a long journey and I was reading this book, a thing called *Good Morning Midnight.* Have you read it?'

'No.'

'All the time I was trying to concentrate, not to listen to the soldier's conversation. They were drinking beer and the table was crowded with bottles and they were getting louder all the time. I reached this part in the book — ahh, she's a beautiful writer — there's this point in the book where the woman loses her baby at birth. This totally lonely person, without one belonging to her in the world, loses her baby, the only thing that gave her any hope — and I just choked up reading it. You know the way tears well up but don't spill and then you can't read?'

Although I have a real love of literature I have never experienced what he talked about and, even though a bit suspicious of that kind of reaction, I nodded in agreement.

'To stop the tears I just put my head back and one soldier said to the other, "What's a five letter word for gristle?" ' Hugo paused to watch me. 'It's all there in the juxtaposition,' he said.

There was nothing I could say.

'Of course that's not what the novel is about. It's the *kind* of thing I hope is happening all through it.' He was still nodding his head as if in disbelief that such a perfect thing could have happened and he was the partaker and witness of it. After this and some more drink either he became incoherent or I ceased to take in what he was saying.

On the way home, dizzy with drink and Hugo's novel under my arm I was annoyed at myself for trying to think of a five letter word for 'gristle'.

That night I did not dare read the book because I knew I was in no fit state to make a judgement. I did, however, look at it. It was a huge fat cash accounts ledger ruled in red and blue covered in Hugo's tiny copperplate handwriting. The colour of the ink varied from page to page, some black, some blue, some red. Occasionally there were words crossed out and corrections inserted above but I did not permit myself to read these. I left the book at my bedside and went to sleep.

I was tempted to quote some passages of the novel here but after deep consideration I have decided against it. It was all too embarrassingly bad. He had not even grasped the first principles of good writing. I would be doing him a further disservice to parade them before the public to laugh at. Some of his ideas were good enough but the way he expressed them was lamentable. One could not even say that it was avant-garde and that I was too stodgy a critic to see it. I know enough about literature not to make a mistake like that.

My problem, over the next weeks, grew into an obsession of what to say to Hugo. I had promised him to be honest yet had not the heart to be cruel. Neither could I be dishonest. This, to me, would have been a far greater cruelty. So I compromised.

After I told him, as kindly as I could, what I thought of his novel, suggesting possible ways to improve it, he seemed to shun my company. Every time I called he was not in. Once or twice I spotted him at a distance in the centre of town but he would slip away like a ghost before I could catch him.

A year must have passed before I talked to him again. I was on my usual Saturday afternoon browse through the book-shops. I was in Green's Second-hand Department, feeling my usual annoyance at the lack of classification of their books. My eyes skimmed from one shelf to another, ton upon ton of print, none of it — not a single name familiar to me. Then suddenly through the shelves I saw Hugo and our eyes met for a fraction of a second. When I went round the other side he was just on the point of leaving. I called him and he stopped. He seemed affable enough but somehow detached from all that was going on around him. He told me that he had left his job in the hospital. They were always picking on him and did not give him his rightful status so he told them what they could do with their job. I asked him to go for a drink but he refused, saying that he no longer indulged. I myself think it was because he had no money.

I had been lecturing for several years when I saw him for the last time. Again he could not avoid me. I saw his familiar gaberdine ahead of me in a crowd of shoppers. His shape had slumped and he walked as if looking for something on the pavement. He walked slower than the crowd so that they flowed past him on either side. I came up behind him — I felt I should — and greeted him. He looked up startled that some-one from the crowd should address him. Then, recognizing me, he smiled.

'How's things?' I asked.

'Not so bad, struggling on.'

He looked terrible — dirty, unshaven. His shirt was filthy and the collar wings curled. His glasses were mended at the bridge of his nose with sticking plaster.

'Are you working?' I knew the answer but felt I had to ask the question.

'No. Not just at the moment.'

I walked along with him and asked him what he was doing now.

'Making raspberry ruffles.'

'What?'

Something of his old intensity returned as he told me about his new hobby of sweet-making. Toffees, macaroons, yellow-man and now he was looking for the ingredients to make raspberry ruffles. Did I know where he could buy loose coconut? No, I said, I didn't. We stood facing each other in the street with nothing to say.

'Doing any writing this weather?' I asked him. He laughed, scoffed almost.

'No — I'm finished with all that long ago.' He made to move away from me.

'But you shouldn't,' I said. 'By all means keep it up. You shouldn't throw a gift away. The last thing I wanted to do was to discourage you.'

He looked at me straight, his eyes hard and needle-like. 'If you say so,' and he walked away into the crowd.

It was about a year after this, as well as I can calculate, that I was sitting reading in my study. Distantly I heard the phone ring and my mother answer it. She came up the stairs and knocked lightly on the door.

'Come in.'

'I've just heard bad news,' she said. She was on the verge of tears.

'What's happened?'

'Poor Hugo is dead.' I was silent for a long time looking at my book, the print jumping before my eyes.

'What happened?'

'The poor thing took his own life. He was found hung in a barn — somewhere outside Dungannon.'

'Jesus. When's th... th... the funeral?'

'All this happened a couple of months ago. He was dead a fortnight when they found him.'

I closed the book and tried to comfort my mother who was very upset and was now crying openly.

I still experience a sense of shock when I remember that day. Of not eating, of being unable to read. I couldn't help feeling that I could have done something to avert the tragedy. I could have called on him, sought him out, perhaps even given him some hope. My only consolation was that during our talk on Paul's wedding day, Paul said that he felt exactly the same way, but he too had done nothing about it. When I asked him if he had ever seen the novel he said no — so far as he knew Hugo had never showed it to anyone. We drank our beer and talked, more like people at a funeral than a wedding, laughing but not loudly enough to betray ourselves to each other.

A Pornographer Woos

I am sitting on the warm sand with my back to a rock watching you, my love. You have just come from a swim and the water is still in beads all over you, immiscible with the suntan oil. There are specks of sand on the thickening folds of your waist. The fine hairs on your legs below the knee are black and slicked all the one way with the sea. Now your body is open to the sun, willing itself to a deeper brown. You tan well by the sea. Your head is turned away from the sun into the shade of your shoulder and occasionally you open one eye to check on the children. You are wearing a black bikini. Your mother says nothing but it is obvious that she doesn't approve. Stretch-marks, pale lightning flashes, descend into your groin.

Your mother sits rustic between us in a print dress. She wears heavy brogue shoes and those thick lisle stockings. When she crosses her legs I can see she is wearing pink bloomers. She has never had a holiday before and finds it difficult to know how to act. She is trying to read the paper but what little breeze there is keeps blowing and turning the pages. Eventually she folds the paper into a small square and reads it like that. She holds the square with one hand and shades her glasses with the other.

Two of the children come running up the beach with that curious quickness they have when they run barefoot over ribbed sand. They are very brown and stark naked, something we know again is disapproved of, by reading their grandmother's silence. They have come for their bucket and spade because they have found a brown ogee thing and they want to bring it and show it to me. The eldest girl, Maeve, runs away becoming incredibly small until she reaches the water's edge. Anne, a year younger, stands beside me with her Kwashiorkor tummy. She has forgotten the brown ogee and is examining something on the rock behind my head. She says 'bloodsuckers' and I turn round. I see one, then look to the side and see another and another. They are all over the rock, minute, pin-point, scarlet spiders.

Maeve comes back with the brown ogee covered with seawater in the bucket. It is a sea-mat and I tell her its name. She contorts and says it is horrible. It is about the size of a child's hand, an elliptical mound covered with spiky hairs. I carry it over to you and you open one eye. I say, 'Look.' Your mother becomes curious and says, 'What is it?' I show it to you, winking with the eye farthest from her but you don't get the allusion because you too ask, 'What is it?' I tell you it is a sea-mat. Maeve goes off waving her spade in the air.

I have disturbed you because you sit up on your towel, gathering your knees up to your chest. I catch your eye and it holds for infinitesmally longer than as if you were just looking. You rise and come over to me and stoop to look in the bucket. I see the whiteness deep between your breasts. Leaning over, your hands on your knees, you raise just your eyes and look at me from between the hanging of your hair. I pretend to talk, watching your mother, who turns away. You squat by the bucket opening your thighs towards me and purse your mouth. You say, 'It is hot,' and smile, then go maddeningly back to lie on your towel.

I reach over into your basket. There is an assortment of children's clothes, your underwear bundled secretly, a squash-bottle, sun-tan lotion and at last — my jotter and biro. It is a small jotter, the pages held by a wire spiral across the top. I watch you lying in front of me shining with oil. When you lie your breasts almost disappear. There are some hairs peeping at your crotch. Others, lower, have been coyly shaved. On the inside of your right foot is the dark varicose patch which came up after the third baby.

I begin to write what we should, at that minute, be doing. I have never written pornography before and I feel a conspicuous bump appearing in my bathing trunks. I laugh and cross my legs and continue writing. As I come to the end of the second page I have got the couple (with our own names) as far as the hotel room. They begin to strip and caress. I look up and your mother is looking straight at me. She smiles and I smile back at her. She knows I write for a living. I am working. I have just peeled your pants beneath your knees. I proceed to make us do the most fantastical things. My mind is pages ahead of my pen. I can hardly write quickly enough.

At five pages the deed is done and I tear the pages off from the spiral and hand them to you. You turn over and begin to read.

This flurry of movement must have stirred your mother because she comes across to the basket and scrabbles at the bottom for a packet of mints. She sits beside me on the rock, offers me one which I refuse, then pops one into her mouth. For the first time on the holiday she has overcome her shyness to talk to me on her own. She talks of how much she is enjoying herself. The holiday, she says, is taking her out of herself. Her hair is steel-grey darkening at the roots. After your father's death left her on her own we knew that she should get away. I have found her a woman who hides her emotion as much as she can. The most she would allow herself was to tell us how, several times, when she got up in the morning she had put two eggs in the pot. It's the length of the day, she says, that gets her. I knew she was terrified at first in the dining room but now she is getting used to it and even criticises the slowness of the service. She has struck up an aquaintance with an old priest whom she met in the sitting-room. He walks the beach at low tide, always wearing his hat and carries a rolled pac-a-mac in one hand.

I look at you and you are still reading the pages. You lean on your elbows, your shoulders high and, I see, shaking with laughter. When you are finished you fold the pages smaller and smaller, then turn on your back and close your eyes without so much as a look in our direction.

Your mother decides to go to the water's edge to see the children. She walks with arms folded, unused to having nothing to carry. I go over to you. Without opening your eyes you tell me I am filthy, whispered even though your mother is fifty yards away. You tell me to burn it, tearing it up would not be safe enough. I feel annoyed that you haven't taken it in the spirit in which it was given. I unfold the pages and begin to read it again. The bump reinstates itself. I laugh at some of my artistic attempts — 'the chittering noise of the venetian blinds', 'luminous pulsing tide' — I put the pages in my trousers pocket on the rock.

Suddenly Anne comes running. Her mouth is open and screaming. Someone has thrown sand in her face. You sit upright, your voice incredulous that such a thing should happen to your child. Anne, standing, comes to your shoulder. You wrap your arms round her nakedness and call her 'Lamb' and 'Angel' but the child still cries. You take a tissue from your bag and lick one corner of it and begin to wipe the sticking sand from round her eyes. I watch your face as you do this. Intent, skilful, a beautiful face focused on other-than-me. This, the mother of my children. Your tongue licks out again wetting the tissue. The crying goes on and you begin to scold lightly giving the child enough confidence to stop. 'A big girl like you?' You take the child's cleaned face into the softness of your neck and the tears subside. From the basket miraculously you produce a mint and then you are both away walking, you stooping at the waist to laugh on a level with your child's face.

You stand talking to your mother where the glare of the sand and the sea meet. You are much taller than she. You come back to me covering half the distance in a stiff-legged run. When you reach the rock you point your feet and begin pulling on your jeans. I ask where you are going. You smile at me out of the head hole of your T-shirt, your midriff bare and say that we are going back to the hotel.

'Mammy will be along with the children in an hour or so.'
'What did you tell her?'
'I told her you were dying for a drink before tea.'

We walked quickly back to the hotel. At first we have an arm around each other's waist but it is awkward, like a three-legged race, so we break and just hold hands. In the hotel room there are no venetian blinds but the white net curtains belly and fold in the breeze of the open window. It is hot enough to lie on the coverlet.

It has that special smell by the sea-side and afterwards in the bar as we sit, slaked from the waist down, I tell you so. You smile and we await the return of your mother and our children.

A Present for Christmas

McGettigan woke in the light of midday, numb with the cold. He had forgotten to close the door the night before and his coat had slipped off him onto the boards of the floor. He swivelled round on the sofa and put the overcoat on, trying to stop shivering. At his feet there was a dark green wine bottle and his hand shook as he reached out to test its weight. He wondered if he had had the foresight to leave a drop to warm himself in the morning. It was empty and he flung it in the corner with the others, wincing at the noise of the crash.

He got to his feet and buttoned the only button on his coat. The middle section he held together with his hands thrust deep in his pockets and went out into the street putting his head down against the wind. He badly needed something to warm him.

His hand searched for his trouser pocket without the hole. There was a crumpled pound and what felt like a fair amount of silver. He was all right. Nobody had fleeced him the night before. Yesterday he had got his Christmas money from the Assistance and he had what would cure him today, with maybe something left for Christmas Day itself.

Strannix's bar was at the back of the Law Courts about two minutes from McGettigan's room but to McGettigan it seemed like an eternity. His thin coat flapped about his knees. He was so tall he always thought he got the worst of the wind. When he pushed open the door of the bar he felt the wave of heat and smoke and spirit smells surround him like a hug. He looked quickly behind the bar. Strannix wasn't on. It was only the barman, Hughie — a good sort. McGettigan went up to the counter and stood shivering. Hughie set him up a hot wine without a word. McGettigan put the money down on the marble slab but Hughie gestured it away.

'Happy Christmas, big lad,' he said. McGettigan nodded still unable to speak. He took the steaming glass, carrying it in both hands, to a bench at the back of the bar, and waited a moment until it cooled a bit. Then he downed it in one. He felt his insides unfurl and some of the pain begin to disappear. He got another one which he paid for.

After the second the pains had almost gone and he could unbend his long legs, look up and take in his surroundings. It was past two by the bar clock and there was a fair number in the bar. Now he saw the holly and the multi-coloured decorations and the HAPPY XMAS written white on the mirror behind the bar. There was a mixture of people at the counter, locals and ones in from the Law Courts with their waistcoats and sharp suits. They were wise-cracking and laughing and talking between each other which didn't happen every day of the year. With Strannix off he could risk going up to the bar. You never know what could happen. It was the sort of day a man could easily get drink bought for him.

He stood for a long time smiling at their jokes but nobody took any notice of him so he bought himself another hot wine and went back to his seat. It was funny how he'd forgotten that it was so near Christmas. One day was very much the same as another. Long ago Christmases had been good. There had been plenty to eat and drink. A chicken, vegetables and spuds, all at the same meal, ending up with plum-duff and custard. Afterwards the Da, if he wasn't too drunk, would serve out the mulled claret. He would heat a poker until it glowed red and sparked white when bits of dust hit it as he drew it from the fire — that was another thing, they'd always had a fire at Christmas — then he'd plunge it down the neck of the bottle and serve the wine out in cups with a spoonful of sugar in the bottom of each. Then they knew that they could go out and play with their new things until midnight if they liked, because the Ma and the Da would get full and fall asleep in their chairs. By bedtime their new things were always broken but it didn't seem to matter because you could always do something with them. Those were the days.

But there were bad times as well. He remembered the Christmas day he ended lying on the cold lino, crying in the corner, sore from head to foot after a beating the Da had given him. He had knocked one of the figures from the crib on the mantlepiece and it smashed to white plaster bits on the hearth. The Da had bought the crib the day before and was a bit the worse for drink and he had laid into him with the belt — buckle and all. Even now he couldn't remember which figure it was.

McGettigan was glad he wasn't married. He could get full whenever he liked without children to worry about. He was his own master. He could have a good Christmas. He searched his pockets and took out all his money and counted it. He could afford a fair bit for Christmas Day. He knew he should get it now, just in case, and have it put to one side. Maybe he could get something to eat as well.

He went up to the counter and Hughie leaned over to hear him above the noise of the bar. When McGettigan asked him for a carry-out Hughie reminded him that it was only half-past two. Then McGettigan explained that he wanted it for Christmas. Three pint bottles of stout and three of wine.

'Will this do?' asked Hughie holding up the cheapest wine in the place and smiling. He put the bottles in a bag and left it behind the counter.

'You'll tell the boss it's for me, if he comes in,' said McGettigan.

'If Strannix comes in you'll be out on your ear,' Hughie said.

Strannix was a mean get and everybody knew it. He hated McGettigan, saying that he was the type of customer he could well do without. People like him got the place a bad name. What he really meant was that the judges and lawyers, who drank only the dearest and best — and lots of it — might object to McGettigan's sort. Strannix would strangle his grandmother for a halfpenny. It was a standing joke in the bar for the lawyers, when served with whiskey, to say, 'I'll just put a little more water in this.' Strannix was an out-and-out crook.

98

He not only owned the bar but also the houses of half the surrounding streets. McGettigan paid him an exorbitant amount for his room and although he hated doing it he paid as regularly as possible because he wanted to hold onto this last shred. You were beat when you didn't have a place to go. His room was the last thing he wanted to lose.

Now that he was feeling relaxed McGettigan got himself a stout and as he went back to his seat he saw Judge Boucher come in. Everybody at the bar wished him a happy Christmas in a ragged chorus. One young lawyer having wished him all the best, turned and rolled his eyes and sniggered into his hot whiskey.

Judge Boucher was a fat man, red faced with a network of tiny broken purple veins. He wore a thick, warm camel-hair overcoat and was peeling off a pair of fur-lined gloves. McGettigan hadn't realized he was bald the first time he had seen him because then he was wearing his judge's wig and sentencing him to three months for drunk and disorderly. McGettigan saw him now tilt his first gin and tonic so far back that the lemon slice hit his moustache. He slid the glass back to Hughie who refilled it. Judge Boucher cracked and rubbed his hands together and said something about how cold it was, then he pulled a piece of paper from his pocket and handed it to Hughie with a wad of money. The judge seemed to be buying for those around him so McGettigan went up close to him.

'How're ye Judge,' he said. McGettigan was a good six inches taller that the judge, but round shouldered. The judge turned and looked up at him.

'McGettigan. Keeping out of trouble, eh?' he said.

'Yis, sur. But things is bad at the minute . . . like . . . you know how it is. Now if I had the money for a bed . . .' said McGettigan fingering the stubble of his chin.

'I'll buy you no drink,' snapped the judge. 'That's the cause of your trouble, man. You look dreadful. How long is it since you've eaten?'

'It's not the food your lordship . . .' began McGettigan but he was interrupted by the judge ordering him a meat pie. He took it with mumbled thanks and went back to his seat once again.

'Happy Christmas,' shouted the judge across the bar.

Just then Strannix came in behind the bar. He was a huge muscular man and had his sleeves rolled up to his biceps. He talked in a loud Southern brogue. When he spied McGettigan he leaned over the bar hissing, 'Ya skinney big hairpin. I thought I told you if ever I caught you . . .'

'Mr Strannix,' called the judge from the other end of the counter. Strannix's face changed from venom to smile as he walked the duck-boards to where the judge stood.

'Yes Judge what can I do for you?' he said. The judge had now become the professional.

'Let him be,' he said. 'Good will to all men and all that.' He laughed loudly and winked in McGettigan's direction. Strannix filled the judge's glass again and stood with a fixed smile waiting for the money.

At four o'clock the judge's car arrived for him and after much handshaking and backslapping he left. McGettigan knew his time had come. Strannix scowled over at him and with a vicious gesture of his big thumb, ordered him out.

'Hughie has a parcel for me,' said McGettigan defiantly, '. . . and it's paid for,' he added before Strannix could ask. Strannix grabbed the paper bag, then came round the counter and shoved it into McGettigan's arms and guided him firmly out the door. As the door closed McGettigan shouted, 'I hope this Christmas is your last.'

The door opened again and Strannix stuck his big face out. 'If you don't watch yourself I'll be round for the rent,' he snarled.

McGettigan spat on the pavement loud enough for Strannix to hear.

It was beginning to rain and the dark sky seemed to bring on the night more quickly. McGettigan clutched his carry-out in the crook of his arm, his exposed hand getting cold. Then he sensed something odd about the shape in the bag. There was a triangular shape in there. Not a shape he knew.

He stopped at the next street light and opened the bag. There was a bottle of whiskey, triangular in section. There was also a bottle of vodka, two bottles of gin, a bottle of brandy and what looked like some tonic.

He began to run as fast as he could. He was in bad shape, his breath rasped in his throat, his boots were filled with lead, his heart moved up and thumped in his head. As he ran he said a frantic prayer that they wouldn't catch him.

Once inside his room he set his parcel gently on the sofa, snibbed the door and lay against it panting and heaving. When he got his breath back he hunted the yard, in the last remaining daylight for some nails he knew were in a tin. Then he hammered them through the door into the jamb with wild swings of a hatchet. Then he pushed the sofa against the door and looked around the room. There was nothing else that could be moved. He sat down on the floor against the wall at the window and lined the bottles in front of him. Taking them out they tinked like full bells. In silence he waited for Strannix.

Within minutes he came, he and Judge Boucher stamping into the hallway. They battered on the door, shouting his name. Strannix shouted, 'McGettigan. We know you're in there. If you don't come out I'll kill you.'

The judge's voice tried to reason. 'I bought you a meat pie, McGettigan.' He sounded genuinely hurt.

But his voice was drowned by Strannix.

'McGettigan, I know you can hear me. If you don't hand back that parcel I'll get you evicted.' There was silence. Low voices conferred outside the door. Then Strannix shouted again. 'Evicted means put out, you stupid hairpin.'

Then after some more shouting and pummelling on the door they went away, their mumbles and footsteps fading gradually.

McGettigan laughed as he hadn't laughed for years, his head thrown back against the wall. He played eeny-meeny-miney-mo with the bottles in front of him — and the whiskey won. The click of the metal seal breaking he thought much nicer than the pop of a cork. He teased himself by not drinking immediately but got up and, to celebrate, put a shilling in the meter to light the gas fire. Its white clay sections were broken and had all fallen to the bottom. The fire banged loudly because it had not been lit for such a long time, making him jump back and laugh.

Then McGettigan pulled the sofa up to the fire and kicked off his boots. His toes showed white through the holes in his socks and the steam began to rise from his feet. A rectangle of light fell on the floor from the streetlamp outside the uncurtained window. The whiskey was red and gold in the light from the fas fire.

He put the bottle to his head and drank. The heat from inside him met the warmth of his feet and they joined in comfort. Again and again he put the bottle to his head and each time he lowered it he listened to the music of the back-slop. Soon the window became a bright diamond and he wondered if it was silver rain drifting in the halo of the lamp or if it was snow for Christmas. Choirs of boy sopranos sang carols and McGettigan, humming, conducted slowly with his free hand and the room bloomed in the darkness of December.

Anodyne

James Delargy sat in the corner at the small table with the one place-setting which the girl had indicated. She set the typed menu in its plastic casing in front of him and went off to lean against the side-board. There was a typing error, a percentage mark between '19' and 'July'. He propped the menu against the silver milk jug, dented and worn through to the yellow brass. When the waitress came back he ordered a mixed grill. She was not good-looking but had a nice face when she smiled. The table cloth was white starched linen, clean except for one small stain with tomato seeds embedded in it. He picked up a knife and scraped the seeds from the cloth.

Three elderly priests or Christian Brothers came in, men with thin collars, and sat at a table in an alcove. At least one of them must be interesting, thought James. The eldest one with white hair looked a bit like Auden — his face all cracked and wrinkled. But he had been sadly disappointed in priests before. Not all of them were well read. His mixed grill came.

'Do you do this all year round?' James asked her.

'Ach no, just for the summer,' she said. Her accent was pleasant and lilting.

'Are you a student?' he asked.

'Are you daft? Me, a student. I can hardly add two and two.'

'Oh I see.'

'There is no work around here in the winter. I go to Scotland to the factories. There is plenty of work there.' As she went back to the kitchen James noticed that her legs were very thick and that half an inch of her slip was showing beneath her black dress.

After tea he took a rolled pacamac and walked out to explore the town. It wasn't much more than one street with a few smaller ones running off it. Most of the shop windows were full of holiday trinkets and picture postcards. He called in the biggest of these to see if there was any books. He had been foolish enough not to bring anything with him and the only reading he could get at the station had been *Howards End*. It had been a long time since he had read it. The shop was dark, hung about with Aran sweaters and bales of Irish tweed. There was a glass counter full of gnomes and shamrock-covered ashtrays. A rack of postcards that swung round. Against the back of the shop was a small book-shelf. He moved to it and began to read the titles on the spines of the books. A girl of about eight came out of the curtain covered kitchen.

'Yes?' she said.

'I'm just looking.' The girl stood on as if he wasn't to be trusted. There was nothing but Dennis Wheatleys and Agatha Christies, science fiction and love paperbacks. There was another copy of *Howards End* and he smiled to himself. The only thing he could get was a Hemingway. He paid the girl who waited till he was out of the shop before she went back into the kitchen.

He walked the length of the beach but was stopped by a large triangular outcrop of rock jutting into the sea. He sat down and watched the water come sluicing in, higher and higher up the beach until it was at his feet. He liked what he had seen of the place — not bad for having been picked at random. The only place the doctor had told him to avoid was the place his mother had brought him for the past twenty years. He said there would be too many memories. 'Go away — get yourself a nice girl. Fall in love and then come back and see me.' The doctor said what he had to do was not to forget, but to use discretion and reason in remembering her. He must begin to build a new life for himself which his mother would have no part in. He must begin to see himself as an adult. He had protested that nursing his mother through that last terrible year would make an adult of anybody. Teaching through the day, sitting up most of the night, putting her on the commode, feeding her, caring for her, watching death insinuate itself into her face. Her nose sharpened like a pencil, her mouth caved in without her teeth those last four days she took to die. The only time he cried was the night she died. It was her total helplessness, hardly able to grip his hand, her sagging jaw, her total lack of dignity as she grunted and gasped for each breath. He thought of her as she was when he was a child and he crushed her slack yellow head against his cheek and cried. He tried to remember the name of the character in Camus's book who went to the pictures the day his mother died. Later he killed an Arab. But he couldn't remember — even now as he sat on the rock he couldn't remember. He was feeling too hot again and he bent to the sea at his feet and splashed his sweating forehead with water. A wave came in and covered his shoes.

He saw that soon the sea would cut him off so he moved back across the beach. The water, flecked and layered with black and gold and yellow reminded him of some of the Impressionists.

Back at the hotel he went up to his room to unpack his things. His room had a small bay window with the curtains hung across the spine of the D. A wardrobe, a dressing table with rosette handles, one of which came off in his hand when he pulled it. The drawer was floored with a page of *The Donegal Democrat*. Stooped over he read a report of a Gaelic match and laughed at the flowery parochial style. He'd had better compositions from his own lads. The carpet was threadbare and nosed its way into an old fireplace blocked by another page of newspaper. In one corner was a wash-hand basin which gulped and gurgled when anybody else in the house used theirs. High up on the wall was a black picture hook.

He packed what clothes he had neatly into the drawer. A fly bizzed at the bay window. He looked round for something to kill it with but could find nothing so he opened the window and shooed it out with his hand. If his mother had been there she'd have dealt with it in her own way. She hated flies. Her love of cleanliness was so surgical that she couldn't bear one in the room with her. One day when he was cleaning out the fire he went to the bin with ashes and found his only copy of *Death in Venice* lying on top of the potato peelings and bacon rinds. He picked it up and walked back into the house holding the book between his finger and thumb.

'Mother,' he yelled. 'Did you throw my *Death in Venice* in the bin?' He held up the book.

'I don't know. I might have.'

'In under God, *why*?'

'I killed a fly with it.'

James looked closely at the cover. There was a small red splash.

'Why do you kill flies with my books?'

'It must have the nearest thing to hand at the time.' She shuddered. 'Horrible big buzzer.'

'Why don't you use the paper?' She didn't answer. 'Mother, sometimes you are incredible.'

'Such a fuss over an old paperback,' she muttered.

'It's *Death in Venice*.'

'It's all germs now.'

'I swear if you do it again, I'll leave. Get a flat of my own somewhere.' He walked out and wiped the cover with a damp cloth dipped in disinfectant. How many times had she done that? There were so many of his books missing even though he had made a firm rule never to lend them. Maybe that's where they were going. Into the bin. His mother had been hard to stick at times. He must stop thinking about her. Again he was feeling too hot. He filled the wash basin. The water was yellow-brown. It must be the turf. Small streams all over the bogs, 'glue-gold' was the colour of them. Invariably Hopkins found the right word. He splashed the cold water into his face.

There were other times when she was unforgettable, when he thought her the most beautiful woman in the world. He could sit and listen to her all night when she was entertaining guests. She talked to and questioned them with such quiet concern. She talked to them as if she loved them, as if she had singled them out from the common herd.

Many nights when they were on their own she would sit with one leg beneath her, always embroidering, and talk of her own girlhood. Of the big house in which she had lived, her mother's dress hissing on the hallway, the place full of Italians visiting from the Dublin Opera, of silver soup tureens, of nannies and cooks and servants. Late in life when, as she said herself, nobody else would take her, she fell for a whiskey traveller who was a Catholic. Her family disowned her. He was a handsome man and his oval photograph, with his Bismarck moustache and butterfly collar still hung on the wall beside her bed. Then, she said, he became his own best customer.

A thing that he could never understand about her was that she loved books but didn't respect them. She told him of an anthology of poetry she'd been given and of how each day she would go a long walk she would tear out several pages to take with her, being too lazy, she said, to cart the whole book about the countryside. He felt a lump in his throat and a hotness in his eyes as he thought of the neverness of her. He would *never* see her again. He must buy a hat tomorrow if it was warm and sunny. His bald spot became intolerably tender if he got it sunburned.

During tea he studied the faces around the dining room. He decided that he would have to make the effort to be sociable. On his way out he went to the table where the Brothers sat in the alcove.

'Excuse me, could I buy you a drink after your meal?' The biggest of the three raised his hands and laughed.

'Ah no thank you very much but we don't drink.' He had the flattest of Dublin accents. The others nodded in agreement. James bowed slightly and could think of nothing more to say. He went out into the bar himself. He was no good at this sort of thing. His mother had always made the approaches. She had an unerring instinct for choosing the right people. You could see them warming to her immediately as she began to talk. The Brothers would never have refused her if she had asked them. But would she have asked them? Probably not, with her instinct.

James ordered a beer. There was a man sitting reading a book at the far side of the bar. He had the book flat on his knees so that the cover was hidden. James took his drink and

107

sat at the table next to him. He sipped his beer. The man read on, not looking up.

'Do you read much?' James asked.

'No. Not at all. Holidays mostly. Sometimes at night I'll read a bit if I can't get to sleep. It helps put me over.'

'Yes,' said James. 'What's the book?' The man showed him the cover. It was an American sex novel. A picture of a blonde in her slip with one foot on a chair so that you could see her stocking tops and the v of her lace panties.

'It was all I could get down here,' he said. 'Are you on holiday?'

James nodded and swallowed his beer.

'Will you have another?' said the man half rising out of his seat.

'No. No thanks, I must be off,' James answered quickly. 'How long are you staying?'

'Another week,' said the man.

'Then I'll see you around.'

As James moved past the bar the manager put his head round the door and said in an undertone to the barman, 'John, you'll not forget the bottle of Powers for the Brothers' room.'

James walked out of town but the landscape was the same as far as the eye could see. A scatter of grey one-storey houses against the grey-green of the poor land. Networks of low stone walls fenced fields which were full of rocks themselves. He turned back seeing no variety and went back to his room to read Hemingway. At eleven he took his sleeping pill and fell asleep almost immediately. The last thing he saw was the picture hook above the mantelpiece, caught in a shaft of light from the street where the curtains did not quite meet.

'Cheapskates,' he thought, a favourite word of his mother's.

The next day he walked along the beach close to the water's edge. The tide was out and he discovered that he could walk past the rocks which had stopped him the previous night. After about a mile he came to another high projection of rock topped by tufted grass with a ravine at its centre. Round the corner of the rock he saw a girl squatting. He ducked back then peeped out again to watch her. She was sitting on a rock drawing. Her long legs were bare and half folded under her. Her hair was yellow. He hesitated a moment then decided to walk close past her to get a better look. He walked casually, his hands behind his back, looking out to sea and when he came level with her he glanced round. She smiled at him, guilty of her sketch book.

'Hello,' she greeted him. James stopped and went towards her. Close up he noticed that her midriff was bare, her blouse knotted beneath her breasts.

'Sketching?' he asked.

'Yes,' she said, throwing her arm over her drawing just as one of the boys in his class would do. 'Please don't look.'

'It's a lovely morning,' he said but felt it too banal a thing to say, so he added, '. . . for sketching. The light . . . it's just right.'

'Oh you know about things like that,' she said, starting up. 'Are you an artist?'

James smiled and edged his hip onto a rock. 'No . . . no I'm not.'

She was very beautiful, the more he looked at her. Pure skin, little or no make-up, blonde hair tied back, some strands of which had come loose and fallen down the side of her face. She wore a pink blouse and from where he sat above her he could see the slight curvature which began her breast. Her legs had the faintest trace of pale hair against the sunburned skin.

'May I see?' James asked. She laughed embarrassed, and said that it was absolutely useless. Her accent had class about it, not Northern, but definitely class.

'I'll show you because I've only started,' she said and opened the book. The page was dark grey for pastel and the line of the outcrop of rock had been sketched in, the line of sea and the far side of the lough.

'It's good,' said James looking at her. She bit her bottom lip.

'Then I'd better leave it like that,' she said laughing. 'I'd only ruin it.'

James handed the book back and asked, 'Are you on holiday?'

'Yes, we're staying at the hotel up there.' She pointed. 'Behind those trees.'

'It looks expensive.'

'Yes but it's gorgeous. An old Georgian mansion. Just the sort of place you'd like to own.'

'Are you staying long?'

She pulled a face. 'We'll be going on Sunday.'

'Who's "we"?'

'I'm here with my parents. That's why I go sketching. There's nothing else to do.'

'You like sketching then?'

'Yes I love things,' she said. She waved her hand in the direction of the sea. '. . . Nature . . . I don't know how to put it. Drawing doesn't really help. If you could somehow get *into* it . . .'

'Have you read Hopkins?' James asked.

'No.' She shook her head from side to side, thinking.

'It's *all* there,' said James. ' "There lives the dearest freshness deep down in things." '

'Oh *him*,' she interrupted. 'Yes I think I have. He's in *The Pageant*.'

'Yes,' said James, left with the rest of the poem inside him.

'Writing poems about it is just a different way of drawing it. It still doesn't help. I don't know. When you like things . . . you're taking in all the time, there's nothing going out. I suppose it has to get out somehow . . . or you'd burst.' She put her hand on her bare midriff as if she had indigestion.

'I don't think it's giving out,' said James. 'It's more a structuring of what we take in. Frost says that poetry is "a momentary stay against confusion".'

'Are you a teacher?' she asked.

'Yes. Does it show that much?'

'*No*. No it's just that you sound so like . . . so clever.'

They both laughed. 'What is there to do at nights here?' James asked.

'Nothing really — sometimes a sing-song in the bar.' She scraped a handful of sand and let it trickle from one hand to the other, then reversed her hands and poured it back again. A joke from an old Bob Hope film came to him.

'This must be where they empty all the old egg-timers.' She laughed appreciatively.

'What's your name?' he asked.

'Rosalind.'

'Mine's James — James Delargy.' He felt he should shake hands but didn't. 'Are there any nice walks about here?'

'Oh yes. The nicest walk is round the foreshore when the tide is out. You can walk for miles and miles.' She smiled up at him and with a finger hooked away a strand of hair which had fallen over her face. 'Would you like me to show you?'

'Yes,' said James. 'Can I see you tonight when the tide is full out again?'

She nodded, smiling happily.

James said, 'It won't be dark till about ten — and we could go for a drink.'

'I'm not . . . I don't drink,' said Rosalind.

'That's OK by me,' said James. 'You can take something.' Again she nodded and clutched her sketch pad to her chest.

'Shall I call up for you at your hotel?'

'No . . . no. I'll come down to you. Where are you staying?' He told her.

'At about eight?'

'Yes.' She put her sketch pad onto her knees. Some of the brown pastel had come off on her blouse. 'Oh look what I've done.' She made a face and tried to dust it off. Her breasts jigged to the touch of her own fingers but the stain remained.

There seemed nothing left to say so James took his leave of her. On his way back to the hotel he lifted a handful of gravelly sand and hurled it at the sea and saw the scatter of small splashes on the water beyond the first wave.

After tea James shaved meticulously and washed his feet in the wash-basin because it had been hot and he had neglected to bring sandals with him. He also looked with concern at his bald patch and saw that it was red. His mother had always said that she didn't know who would look after him when she was gone. He tried to think of Rosalind and how he was going to conduct the evening. She was young and didn't seem to have

111

read very much. He could introduce her to lots of really good stuff. He pulled out the plug and the dirty water sucked away, echoing in all the other rooms of the hotel. He put on cream trousers, a polo necked sweater and slipped the Hemingway into the pocket of his linen jacket. He asked in the kitchen for brown polish and brushed his shoes. The white line of salt where the sea had washed over them disappeared, then he went into the bar to wait. It was a quarter to eight. He wondered if he should wait outside the hotel in case she would be embarrassed about coming into a bar on her own — but on holiday bars were not the same things. At the moment there were children playing around, crawling under tables, squealing and laughing. In a room off the bar a child monotonously played single notes on a piano, while others slid in sock-soles on the small maple dance floor. To pass the time James tried to read a few pages of Hemingway but found he couldn't concentrate.

At eight o'clock the girl from the reception desk came into the bar and looked around. She came over to James and said, 'Mr Delargy?'

'Yes.'

'There is a gentleman at reception to see you.' He followed the girl out. The man waiting there was tall and distinguished looking, grey hair with a small toothbrush moustache.

'Mr Delargy?' James nodded, half gestured to shake hands but seeing no response on the other's part, he stopped. 'May I buy you a drink?'

He was very abrupt. James was confused and followed him without a murmur. In the bar the elder man asked what he drank, then set up a beer and a small whiskey for himself.

'There seems to have been some misunderstanding,' he began. 'I don't want to be nasty about this but I want to be firm. My name is Somerville. I believe you met my daughter Rosalind on the beach this morning.' James nodded. 'I must inform you that my daughter is not yet fifteen and that I do not allow her to go out with boys whom I haven't vetted. I certainly do not permit her to go out unchaperoned with a man of your age. I apologize if I seem offensive but you must see my point of view.'

'I'm sorry, but I didn't realize she was so young,' James stammered.

'I admit she's a big girl for her age. Also it is mostly her fault for not telling you — but she's so naive. She let it slip at tea where she was going and I felt it my duty to come and see you. I hope you don't mind.'

'I . . . I . . . had no idea,' said James. 'She seemed so confident. I knew she was young but not *that* young. I can assure you anyway that she would have been in no danger with me.'

Somerville smiled and relaxed a bit. He drank off half his whiskey.

'She's a very beautiful girl,' said James.

Somerville accepted the remark as a compliment to himself. He drank off the rest of his glass and was about to rise to go saying, 'Thank you Mr Delargy for being so understanding . . .'

'Just a moment,' said James. He was at the bar before Somerville could refuse. He came back with the drinks and they both sat silent for a moment. They both raised their drinks at the same time for something to do.

'I see you're reading Hemingway,' said Somerville.

'Yes,' said James. 'I'd forgotten how good he was.'

'Like an ox talking,' said Somerville laughing.

'His characters may be but he has some very intelligent things to say about literature.'

'I'm joking really,' said Somerville but James went on.

'He says somewhere that what you read becomes part of your experience, if it is good, that is. Good writing must actually seemed to have happened to you. I think that is very perceptive.'

The other nodded. 'Hemingway is not my period. I read him when I was younger but remained unimpressed.'

'What do you do, Mr Somerville?'

'I teach English.'

'Oh so do I.'

'I lecture at Trinity.'

James edged forward on his seat. 'And what is your period?'

'Early seventeenth century.'

'Oh Donne and Herbert and Crawshaw? I love them,' said James excitedly.

'The prose is more my field. That's what I did my Doctorate in. Launcelot Andrewes, Bacon, Browne. Those chaps,' said Somerville. Gradually the parents came in and the children were rounded up from 'the bar room floor. The single notes on the piano stopped and the rest of the conversation proceeded in an air of good humoured and quiet concentration.

It was after twelve when Dr Somerville left to go back to his hotel. James had drunk much more than he had intended and, when he fell into bed, happy to have had such a good night, he did not need to take a sleeping pill. The picture hook seemed somehow bigger, repulsively static on the wall, triangular like a black fly. He closed his eyes and the bed seemed to race backwards. He opened them to stop the sensation. The picture hook throbbed in the shaft of light, annoying him intensely. James got up from bed and stood on the chair, nearly overbalancing, and pulled the curtains so that they met flush and the room was in complete darkness.

The next day he met Mrs Somerville with her husband for coffee, as arranged.

'My dear,' said Mrs Somerville. 'When he hadn't come home by twelve I could have sworn that you'd shot him,' and they all laughed. James thought how sad it was that his mother would never meet these lovely people. He was sure she would have approved.

The Bull With the Hard Hat

It was one of those rare moments when Dick was conscious
of driving. He loved the feeling of the car being completely
under his control. The road twisted and turned on its way to
the top of the mountain. At each bend he moved his weight in
the seat as he turned the wheel — 'and now Emmerson Fittipaldi is a full half minute in front.' He crossed the finishing
line a minute ahead of the others and pulled in at the lay-by
on the mountain top. With the engine switched off the only
sound was the sighing and buffetting of the wind outside the
car. He marked up his book. He had done twenty-four calls
that morning. Not bad by anybody's standards — that is if
they all worked.

He looked at himself in the driving mirror. He was grey
completely — 'Emmerson Fitt-ee-pal-di, how this man at forty-
five manages to keep his place in the world championship
table . . . nay . . . not keep his place . . . but *lead*.' He reached
over the back seat for his lunch. A flask of tea and plastic box
of sandwiches. He opened the box — cheese again. Why
couldn't Margaret use a bit of imagination about sandwiches.
She had work to do — yes — anybody with eight children had
their hands full, but it wasn't unreasonable to ask for an
occasional change from cheese. The other lads on the job
turned up with roast beef and pickle, egg and tomato, and
onion, one even boasted of cucumber and cod's roe. But he
never got anything except eternal pan bread and processed
cheese. Once in a while he would throw these out the window
for the birds and treat himself to a fish supper in one of the

small towns he passed through. He rolled down both windows of the car for a bit of air and began to eat.

His call book lay on the seat beside him. He picked it up and began to read as he chewed his way through the plasticy cheese and bread, so dry that it stuck to the roof of his mouth. There were still too many repeats, indicated by a red X. Far too many. He had hit a very bad patch. The voice of the instructor at the Artificial Insemination school came to him. 'There are three main reasons for failure. Firstly you may not get to the cow at the right time, secondly the quality of the animal and the sperm used, and lastly the skill of the inseminator himself.' Dick counted the number of red X's he had in his book. They were away above average. Everybody expected to get to the cows at the wrong time now and again. By the time some of these stupid farmers got to the phone and got the cow into the barn the heat was off them. Everybody expected to meet up with heifers who didn't produce results the first time. Dick saw more and more that it was himself was to blame. He couldn't figure out what was going wrong. The ultimate insult was when the boss decided you needed to go back to the school for a refresher course. It was a nice way of putting it but it really meant you were no good at your job. It had happened him twice in ten years and if his present record continued it would happen him again very soon. He flung the book down on the seat beside him. His tea tasted of flask. On a good day it was said you could see five counties from the mountain top but to-day it was dull and windy. Some spits of rain began to fall and blow through his open window and he rolled it up. The mist of the coming rain blotted out the far hills at the other side of the valley.

He was surprised to see another car pull in to the lay-by. There was a man and a woman in it and immediately they stopped, they started. Their heads seemed to meet and form one. Gradually their car steamed up and when he could see no more he lost interest. It was a bit much at one o'clock in the day. He was bad enough himself but not that bad.

But it wasn't his fault. He had put the thing fairly and squarely to Margaret and she point blank refused to take the

Pill or any other precaution. 'On your own head be it,' was his attitude now . . . and sure enough six months later she was pregnant again. Her answer was always the same — 'But it's a sin, it's there in black and white, the Pope says so.' If his job was as good as his home record . . . or vice versa everything would be all right, but now more than ever with a ninth child on the way he couldn't afford to loose his job. He settled back in his seat and put his knee up on the steering wheel, eating a chocolate biscuit for dessert. He could dimly see the dark shapes struggling in the other car. Then they stopped. The driver polished a circle for himself in the windscreen and they drove off leaving Dick on his own again.

It would serve Margaret right if he did take one of the girls out of the office up here for a lunchtime snack. He had fancied Carmel this long time. She was young and bright, always clean and smelt beautiful. If she wore anything white it was only for one day, starched, crisp, white. Her tight mini-skirts, tight enough to see the line of her pants, her long graceful legs nearly drove him to distraction. She was good fun too and would allow most of the men occasionally to squeeze her bottom. She would slap their hands away saying, 'I'll tell your Mammy on you,' but she was never seriously angry. Of course Dick knew that it would take more than a squeeze behind the filing cabinets . . . he would have to take her out to dinner some night, somewhere as far away as Fermanagh . . . but even there he knew a lot of people and a lot of people knew him. Carmel, he knew, would cost more than a hot dinner and a few drinks but it would be nice to try and see how much. While he had been thinking he found that the chocolate biscuit had melted in his hand. He put the remainder of it into his mouth and licked his fingers. He thought that Carmel liked him more than any of the other men. Any time they happened to be in the office on their own she had told him private things, nice things about herself. Even when the office was full of people he liked to watch her writing and her long yellowy hair trailing the page. She handled the phone beautifully, as well. She would tilt her head quickly so that the hair would fall away from her ear. Her fingers with the long polished nails held it delicately, the other hand jotting quick notes. Best of all was the way she would look at Dick, speaking to the farmers in her best Civil Service voice, and winking and screwing her pretty face into awful shapes. Every time he used the phone in the office he could smell the delicate perfume that she left on the mouthpiece.

He looked at himself again in the driving mirror. He thought he was fairly handsome for his age . . . except that he hadn't had time to shave that morning . . . he thought he would be attractive to any young girl. Not a seedy middle aged man but a lover, like Rossano Brazzi. The bull with the hard hat — that's what he was known as on most of the farms or just simply the bull man. It was stupid and it annoyed him slightly. He had never worn a hard hat in his life, besides it was just a job like any other when you got used to the more disgusting aspects of it. The long rubber glove, the cow's hot insides, the constant prevailing smell of dung, the muck and clabber yards he had to tramp through. It was either that or home, he didn't know which was worse. It was the noise at home that got him more than anything else. Eight children, the eldest twelve, the youngest a year, all of whom seemed to fight over the slightest thing. A rag doll, a triangle of cheese, whose turn it was to open the potato crisps, who was to be into the bath first — all could end up in a screaming fight with children rolling about the floor, biting and pulling the hair out of one and other. Dick had to scream and yell louder than the rest to get it stopped. It would stop and the only sound was the TV which was always too loud. The children would sit about sullen and whoever Dick had got to with his hand, smacking the first leg he could see, would snuffle quietly in the corner.

'Will somebody turn down the TV.'

'It's *my* turn.'

'*No,* it's *my* turn. You got turning it off last night.'

'Daddy, say it isn't her turn,' and it would all start once again.

On the top of the mountain he was surrounded by quiet. The small bleating of sheep carried for miles, the wind moaning past his window. He could build a hut up here and live like a monk. He threw his crusts out the window and screwed the cup back onto the flask.

With Carmel it would have been so different. They could have had two nice children and she would be there crisp and clean for him when he came home, the house immaculate, the toys tidied away. Instead he knew Margaret would be lying on the sofa, her feet up in the air because of her veins — it was like this when he would come home. The floor, from the doorway in, would be covered with treacherous trucks and wheeled things, dolls without limbs, pieces of jig-saws.

'Dick, I'm absolutely done out. Could you get the children their bread and jam . . . and whatever you like yourself. Don't bother about me, I couldn't face food at the minute,' and they would all gather round the lino covered table and he would butter what seemed endless pan loaves of bread, spread with blackcurrant jam. Some of them would always drop their piece, jam side down on the floor and screech their head off, because they knew it would be a long time before their turn would come again.

'There's a tin of spaghetti there if you would like it,' Margaret would shout from the other room. 'And while you're there would you heat up the baby's bottle for me.' Dick hated spaghetti and the tin had sat in the larder for about three months but Margaret continued to offer it to him every night. Invariably he ended up with a boiled egg and the remains of the children's bread and jam. He hoped that this, their ninth, would be their last. She couldn't go on producing for ever. She was forty-three now . . . and it showed.

He looked at his watch. It was time he was phoning in to the office to get his afternoon calls. There would probably be hundreds . . . enough to sicken him anyway. He knew he could get through them quickly. If there was one thing he *did* know it was his area, every lane, dirt track and by-way . . . he was good at getting the order of his calls right so that he never had to cover the same ground twice. Once when he'd been sick for a fortnight, just for something to do, he'd drawn a map of his area, labelling all the roads and farms over an area of some twenty square miles.

The nearest phone was about three miles away. He hoped it would be Carmel who would answer. It might brighten his afternoon a bit. He switched on the engine, shattering the silence and edged out onto the main road, looking both ways, then raced through the gears, '. . . and after that prolonged pit-stop Emmerson Fittipaldi is a good two minutes behind the leaders. Is it possible that this man can make up the deficit???' He swung the car into a bend and heard the tyres squealing beneath him.

After he left, the lay-by was silent until two hooded crows landed and began to fight over the crusts he had left lying on the gravel.

The Deep End

On the way home in the empty bus the two boys were silent. They sat as usual in separate seats but made no attempt to avoid paying their fare. Paul sat, his damp towel clenched in the crook of his arm, looking down into the street at each stop. At Manor Street Olly knelt up and looked back at him.

'Say nothing to your Ma, for God's sake, Paul. We'd never get going again.'

'I'm not mad about going again — not for a while,' said Paul.

Olly unfurled his bundle and took out his togs and wrung them out, the droplets splashing onto the battened floor.

'Where are you for this afternoon?' he asked.

'Any dough?'

'Naw.' Olly got up and ran down the bus. 'See ya,' he shouted. Halfway down the stairs he stopped and pulled a cigarette out of his top pocket.

'I'll smoke your half for you, Paul.'

'I hope it chokes you,' Paul called after him.

Paul went home and couldn't eat his dinner. He went up to the bedroom and lay for a long time looking at the ceiling. His mother came up and put her head round the door.

'That's the last time you'll go to the baths — your guts full of oul' lime water — and God knows what else. I'm sure they do more than swim in the water.'

Paul suddenly felt his eyes fill with tears. Then he cried hard. His mother came over and put her arms round him, asking incredulously, 'What's wrong, what's wrong with my big man?'

They queued in the hallway and heard the distant echoing

cease. Above them, on the wall, was an Artificial Respiration poster, its reds gone brown in the sun. Dotted lines and arrows showed the right motions. Somebody had drawn tits on the victim's back and added genitals to the man bending over him. Olly stood, one foot flat against the cream tiled wall, the other slanted like a prop.

'Away and ask her how long they'll be,' he said. Paul crushed his way up to the porthole and came back.

'Ten minutes.'

'Time for a feg.' With two fingers Olly dipped into his breast pocket and pulled out a cigarette. He straightened it out and tapped the loose tobacco into place on his thumb nail. 'Smoke one now and the other one after.'

Paul struck the match between the tiles. Olly cupped the flame in his hands, took two quick puffs then closed his fingers round the cigarette. He leaned back against the wall.

'Don't suck the guts out of it.' Olly turned his head away from Paul's reaching hand, taking the last ounce out of it.

'Come on, it'll be red hot,' said Paul grabbing the cigarette from him. He couldn't inhale as deeply as Olly so he blew the smoke down his nose and passed it back.

'What are they?' he asked.

'Parkies,' said Olly.

'They're OK'. Then after a moment Paul asked, 'Do you believe this cancer thing?'

'Naw, sure my Ma and Da both smoke like trains and look at the age they are.'

'Oul' Hennesy smoked and he's dead – fifty a day,' said Paul.

'You've gotta go sometime – where the hell did oul' Hennesy get the money. Fifty a day. Jesis.'

'All the doctors say it,' said Paul.

'Doctors are stupid. My Da was walking around for two weeks with a broken finger and they didn't even know. They had to send him to the hospital before they found out.' Olly tucked in the loose strands of tobacco at the soggy end with his finger.

'Does your Ma still not allow you?' he asked.

'Naw.'

'Mine gave me one yesterday — she said as long as nobody was in it was OK. She says it's better than smoking behind her back.'

'My Ma would do her nut if she knew.'

A small boy nudged Olly and, looking up at him, said, 'Give us your butt.'

'Fuck off, son,' said Olly dropping the remains of the cigarette on the ground and pressing it with a twist of his toe.

'What about clubbing up for currant squares when we get out?' Paul asked.

'From Lizzie's?'

'Yeah, they're dead on.'

'OK,' said Olly. 'How much have we?'

They took out their money and calculated. If bus fares weren't collected that was so much profit, but a keen conductor had to be allowed for. They had enough. Paul licked his lips and growled.

By now the first crowd had begun to come out in ones and twos. White faced, red eyed, some with their togs on their heads, others their hair wet and spiky, they tumbled out, shouting at each other at the tops of their voices. One boy in raggy jeans, both elbows out of his sweater climbed to the top of the turnstile gate, almost to the ceiling and slopped his wet togs down onto the back of his friend's neck.

'Get to hell out of it,' roared the attendant who had just come out. He stood threatening, his fingers hooked in the loops of his belt, brown muscled in a singlet and jeans. He wore black wellingtons with the white canvas rims turned down. He had a tattoo, blue and red on each arm. The boy scuttled down off the gate and crashed out the door. The attendant said something to the girl behind the pay box and the line began to jostle and fight to get through.

Paul shoved his way up to the arched hole in the perspex and pushed his money to the girl. She gave him a ticket, a towel and a pair of trunks. The towel was a freshly laundered dishcloth, still warm with a clean smell, the trunks a double red triangle held together with string. Paul used the Corporation towel for standing on and dried himself with his own soft towel. The gym teacher had told them the worst thing you could get out of the baths was athletes foot and he himself stood on a towel. Paul's mother always harped on about polio.

'If you had to spend the rest of your days in a wheel-chair it would be a dear swim. The ones that swim over there, you never know what homes they've come out of. It's a bad area.'

'But the water's full of chlorine, Ma.'

'Chlorine, chlorine — what's the use of chlorine if you're going to get polio. Eh? Tell me that. Your father's too soft, allowing you. He says the swimming'll make a man out of you but he'll change his tune if it makes a polio victim out of you.'

Both boys ran down the corridor, their heels hollow yet pinging from the ceiling. They raced through the swing doors looking beneath each half door for a box without a pair of feet. They each got a box to themselves at the deep end. Paul climbed up onto the seat so that he could see out as he got stripped. The pool still moved from the previous session. It looked still enough on the surface but the black lane lines snaked too and fro continuously. He hauled off his pullover, shirt and vest as one unit and hung them on the peg. The same with his trousers and drawers. The whole lot hung like somebody deformed, humped with dangling arms.

Suddenly there was a cry smothered by a dull explosion. Paul looked out over the partition and saw a boy at the bottom of his dive, alone in the pool. He looked flat, spread-eagled, his hair middle shaded and smoothed by the water. He breast-stroked to the surface and blew out a farting noise.

'First in.' It was Olly. 'Get a move on, Paul,' he screamed.

Paul hopped about on one leg putting on his black trunks. Then he put the Corporation ones over them, tying the string at the sides. The red and black looked nice. If you *only* wore the Corporation ones your thing kept showing.

He blessed himself, said the first line of an Act of Contrition and went out of the box. He walked jerkily down to the three foot end, holding his elbows. The water splashed out on the sides and was cold underfoot. By now the pool was threshing with swimmers and the noise was deafening.

'Look at the ribs,' screamed Olly's head.

Paul moved down the steps at the three foot mark and stood on the last step, knee deep.

He splashed some water over his shoulders and face. Then he pushed himself off from the side screaming with cold. Paul had just learned to swim. He could breast-stroke a breadth at the shallow end but above four feet he kept close to the bar. Somebody had once told him, 'If you can swim a breadth you can swim a mile,' but he didn't believe it. He stood for a while jumping up and down stirring the water with his hands. Olly swam down to him and they played diving between each other's legs for a while. Then Olly headed off for the high board. Paul half swam, half pulled himself along the bar to the deep end. Olly climbed the steps to the top board, swiping the wet hair from his eyes. Paul treaded water waiting and watching him. When he reached the top he held onto the railing, a boxer in his corner, then ran and launched himself into the air, his heels cocked and fifteen foot down, exploded into the water. He came up beside Paul.

'Come on and try,' he said. 'It's great.'

'Are you mad?'

'You're yella. Once you've done it once, it's dead easy. Come on.' He swam to the steps and Paul followed. They sloshed out of the water and began climbing the ladder. At the top Paul looked down at the squat, upturned faces and held tight to the rail.

'Ready?' Olly asked.

'You go first.'

'Go on, I want to watch you.'

'You go first or I won't go,' said Paul.

Olly ran and disappeared at the end of the wet matting on the board, plummeting out of sight. Paul blessed himself and waited until Olly came up again.

'Are you yella?' He laughed appearing up the ladder. He ran past Paul and jumped again holding his nose. Paul let go the bar and scrambled quickly down the ladder and jumped as high as he could off the side of the pool. The bubbles seethed up his nose and his ears pounded and rumbled. He came up near Olly.

'I did it.' he shouted.

Olly swam over to him and said, 'Good for you. I thought you were chicken. Come on again.'

'Naw,' said Paul. 'Once is enough. What about playing tig?'

But the tig was no use because Olly would dive into the middle of the six foot end and couldn't be caught.

Afterwards Paul stood out on the side to get his breath back. The sour taste of the lime made him wish for his currant square now. It was colder out of the water than in. Goose pimples came out all over his body and the light hairs on his arms stood up. 'You could strike matches on ye,' his father had once said to him at the sea-side. 'It couldn't be good for him,' his mother added, huddled in the depths of her deck chair. Paul stood shivering and listening to the din. Splashing and slamming of dressing box doors mixed with a continuous jagged scream, which echoed and multiplied when flung back from the high glass roof. It started at the beginning of the session and stayed at the same sawing pitch throughout. The long whistle to end the session shrilled and the noise reached a crescendo as everybody plunged in for the last time.

Paul was near his box and felt too cold for a last fling. He pushed the half door shut and spread the cotton towel on the duck-boarding. He began to dry himself slowly. He peeled off his trunks and left them, a wet figure eight, at his feet. He felt alone in the box. The noise was outside, people whistling, shouting jokes, but inside he was safe and insulated. Private. He looked down at himself, at his wisps of hair. He wondered if he would ever have a bush like the gym teachers. 'You're on the verge of life now my dear boys — soon you will become men,' the Redemptorist, his black and white heart pinned to his chest, smiled. 'And I know you will all make very good men — every last one of you.' Paul dried himself and pulled on his drawers trying not to think about it any more. Then suddenly from outside there was a scream, totally different in tone from any of the shouting and larking that was going on.

'Hey mister, mister.'

Paul stood up on the seat and looked out. A boy, half-dressed, was running up and down the side of the pool pointing into it and screaming all the time, *'mister, mister.'* Paul looked and saw a still figure lying on the bottom at the deep end. The attendant raced past his box and plunged in. He scooped the body up off the bottom and swam with it to the side. Another man took it from him, by an arm and a leg. The boy's mouth was black and open. Paul sat down on the seat so he couldn't see. Everything was completely silent now except for one of the boys who was snivelling and crying. Paul dried his feet and put on his socks. He pulled on his trousers and stood up to look out again. In the middle of a quiet crowd of boys the attendant was kneeling, his clothes darkened with the wet. The boy's body was blue-grey and when the attendant did anything with its arms, they flopped. Paul stood down and finished dressing. He whispered over to Olly, 'Will we go?'

'Wait t'see what happens.' Olly, in his vest, hung over the half door.

'Is he dead?' Paul hissed.

'Looks like it,' said Olly.

Paul sat down again. The box was painted dark green. Initials and dates, crude guitar shapes of women with split and tits were carved or drawn on every square inch of space. He began to read them — 'G.B. WUZ HERE' — 'TONY IS A WANKER' — 'BMcK 1955.' He read these things over and over again until in the distance he heard the bray of an ambulance. It drew close and stopped. There were some sweet papers and a few dead matches lodged beneath the struts of the duckboards at his feet. He picked up his togs and very slowly disentangled them from the red ones. Olly came in dressed.

'What's happening?' Paul asked.

'They're away.'

Paul looked out. The crowd had gone and everyone was back in their boxes getting dressed. Someone started to whistle but stopped. The pool was absolutely still now, the black lines at the bottom ruled rigid, perspective straight, the surface a turquoise pane.

They walked straddle-legged down the slippery edge of the pool and threw their borrowed togs and towels into the bin.

Outside at the turnstile the girl had put a piece of cardboard over the porthole and there was a queue, quieter than usual, waiting to see if they were going to get in or not.

The boys walked down the steps and crossed the road to the bus stop at Lizzie's bakery. Olly looked at the currant squares in the window. About a quarter of a trayful had been sold. Then he too leaned his back against the window and the two of them stood, their heads turned, waiting for a bus.